UNCAGED

CORPS SECURITY, NOVELLA 3.5

HARPER SLOAN

Cover Design by MGBookCovers
Editing by Mickey Reed
Formatting by Champagne Formats

ISBN 13: 978-1496145437

ISBN 10: 1496145437

To contact Harper:

Website: www.authorharpersloan.com

Email: authorharpersloan@gmail.com

Facebook: www.facebook.com/harpersloanbooks

UNCAGED PLAYLIST

I And Love And You – The Avett Brothers
Lucky – Jason Mraz
You & I – One Direction
How Long Will I Love You – Ellie Goulding
All of Me – John Legend
Collide – Howie Day
Mine Would Be You – Blake Shelton
Faithfully – Journey
I'll Make Love To You - Boyz II Men
Wherever You Will Go – Charlene Soraia
Gravity – Sara Bareilles
Look at Me – Carrie Underwood
Small Bump – Ed Sheeran
God Gave Me You – Blake Shelton
Make You Feel My Love – Adele

DEDICATION

TO THE GIRLS THAT MAKE UP THE INDIE
ROMANCE AUTHOR CHICKS. FOR KEEPING
ME MOTIVATED, HELPING ME PUSH THROUGH
THE DREADED WRITERS BLOCK, AND MAKING
ME LAUGH WHEN I REALLY JUST WANTED TO
THROW MY COMPUTER AGAINST THE WALL.

AND...FOR TUMBLR INSPIRATIONS

CHAPTER 1

Greg

EARLY SPRING

I'VE BEEN sitting in my truck, staring through out the windshield without seeing a thing. My skin feels tight, my blood too hot, and my heart is beating too fast. The smile on my face though? It feels like it will never leave. Never—not once—did I ever think this would be reachable. When I pictured my future, it was always with the acceptance that I would just be cool Uncle Greg, and maybe if I were lucky, I would find someone compatible enough to spend my life with. I didn't expect love. I had given up that hope years ago.

Then I met Melissa, and everything I could have settled for went flying out the window. Poof—in an instant, I met my future. I crave her. The feelings she gave me and the love I knew would come from her was all that mattered.

We haven't had an easy time of it. There was the time when we almost lost Cohen that I thought I would once again end up with nothing. When I first met Melissa's nephew, Cohen, that boy had me wrapped around his little awesome finger. Melissa and her mom had raised him since his mom—her sister—had passed away. He was her boy. And now? Now he's *our* boy.

We both went through a tough time after Cohen's kidnapping. Not only was there a period when I didn't know if I would get him back, but in the mess of things, we also lost Melissa's mom.

But my girl is strong. We overcame together. My girl… My wife, and our beautiful little boy. And now? Now we have a bright future ahead of us. Nothing could top those two in my life. Not a damn thing.

Until last weekend.

I'll never forget the day she came home from visiting her sister and mother's graves. Normally, that would be something all three of us would do together. Cohen likes to spend time talking to his angels, and I know it gives Melissa some peace to have a place where she feels they are. Somewhere tangible so she can still be with them.

I watch out the corner of my eye when I hear a car pulling into the driveway. Cohen and I were kicking some serious ninja ass, rolling around in the front lawn, and just enjoying some man time. Melissa has been gone for a while now, so I know before even looking at her beautiful face that she's home.

I finally detach Cohen's small body from where we just conquered our last 'bad guy.' Somehow, that fight had turned into a wrestling and tickling match. Hell, I don't care what the reason is. If my little dude is laughing, that's all that matters.

Finally getting loose, I turn and spy Melissa through the windshield. She's been sitting in her car, just watching us with her blinding smile fully in place. My heart picks up speed when I look into her eyes so full of love for her men.

"Life doesn't get any better than this, C-Man."

Cohen turns, his big brown eyes twinkling with happiness. "Yeah it does. If we had some pizza!"

I laugh but turn my attention back to Melissa when I hear the car door shut. Cohen doesn't say anything else, but hell, even he gets stunned silent when she walks into our path.

She takes her time walking over to us. When she gets close enough, Cohen jumps up, runs and gives her a big hug before he starts dancing around the yard in a battle only he understands. His little arms flap around, his legs kick out, and the biggest grin spreads across his face. She doesn't even pause. Instead, she walks right up to me and plops her fine ass down in my lap. My arms wrap around her body, and I pull her against my lap, fighting the urge to throw her down and take her hard.

She laughs, wiggling against my growing erection. Yeah, she knows exactly what she's up to. She turns, her smile lighting up her face, and leans in and kisses me.

Resting her forehead against mine, her eyes still holding her smile, she whispers softly words that touch me to my very soul.

"If it's a girl, maybe we can come up with something to honor both our sisters."

A statement. Not a hypothetical 'if we have one in the future' kind of statement.

I come out of my daze, my smile wide enough that my face hurts, and get ready to climb out of my truck. I know that the second that I step foot into the office the guys will take one look at me and know. They may not know what's got me smiling like an idiot, but they will know something significant has happened. It's not easy keeping something so life changing to myself. But with news like this, I can't wait to share. Hell, I would be screaming from the rafters, taking out ads in the local paper, maybe even a few billboards if I could.

I lock up the truck, and before I can even take a step, I hear him.

"Gregory!"

I smile at Sway and walk over to where he's standing outside of his shop.

"What's going on, Sway?"

"'What's going on,' he says? Oh nothing much, you gorgeous man. Just sitting here, minding my own business, when I see you pull in, park, and just sit there with that delicious smile happening. That's what is happening, Gregory! Blinding me with all that yumminess all the way into my salon."

He's standing there, hands on his hips, tapping one red leather-booted foot, his long blond hair falling over his shoulder and the ever-present naughty gleam in his eyes. No shame at all in the fact that I'm pretty sure he just took all my clothes off as I walked across the parking lot.

"Stop thinking about me naked, Sway," I guffaw. "I got some good news this weekend. You can't wipe this smile off if you tried."

"Oh, Gregory… That sounds like an invitation to try." We both laugh, but truth be told, I doubt there is anything that can knock me off my high. "Well? Are you going to tell Sway what has you all happilicious?"

Happilicious? The hell?

"You're something else, Sway." I laugh, shaking my head. "Melissa told me this weekend that we're pregnant. Well…she's pregnant, but you know what I mean." Even saying it out loud brings a fresh round of pure fucking joy to flush through my system.

My girl. Pregnant.

"Ohhhhh! A baby!" Sway starts going on and on about Uncle Sway this, baby showers that, and that is when I take my cue to leave.

Right when I open my mouth to tell him bye, I hear it. Clapping coming from behind me. Turning, I find them. Axel, Beck, Coop, and Maddox are all clapping like demented seals with smiles front and center. Even Maddox has a grin on his normally stoic face.

"Congratulations, brother. Didn't know it was possible with all those holes and rings you have through your dick," Beck spouts.

"Would have thought with as many as he's rocking, that those little swimmers wouldn't have a chance," laughs Axel.

I start to chuckle until I hear a gasp of pleasure coming from behind me.

"What! Gregory, what is *this*?" I turn to see Sway dramatically fanning his face, his eyes zoned in on my crotch.

Isn't this just lovely. I was apparently wrong; there is something that could wipe the smile clear off my face.

"Nothing, Sway," I say, trying my best for a stern voice while leveling the four morons with my hardest 'shut the fuck up' look.

"Gregory Cage, do you have *piercings*?" he practically pants.

Shit. "Thanks a lot, jackasses," I grind out. They all laugh. Even Maddox is laughing so hard that he has tears in his eyes.

"How far of a stretch is it that you'll forget you heard that?" I ask Sway.

"Oh, darling. I'll forget that juicy piece of yum the day that pigs learn to fly. And to think, I thought you were the straight-laced one of the bunch. Who knew you were hiding all of that?" His eyes roam over my body before landing right on my crotch again.

Jesus Christ.

"Sway, I'm a married man now. Stop thinking about my dick."

Really, as annoyed as I am with the idiots still laughing by the door to our office, Sway's face really is comical. A mix between shock and awe.

"Plus, Maddox has one too. Lust over him. He's single." I laugh before pushing my way through the group. They're all laughing even harder now—except for Maddox.

"Oh my gosh! Congratulations, Greg!" Emmy screams when I walk through the front lobby. She politely ignores the fact that the whole state of Georgia may know about my piercings now. "I bet you, Melissa, and Cohen are thrilled!"

"Thanks, Em. We couldn't be happier." I give her a warm smile and hug. We chat for a few minutes before I continue down the hall. It doesn't take long before the four amigos are filing in. I should have seen it coming. No way they would leave it all at the door. Literally.

"Well?" Coop asks.

"Well, what, asshat?" I throw back before dropping down in my chair.

"Congrats, man. Izzy told me last night," Axel interrupts, at least having the decency not to mention my junk again.

"Well what, my ass. All the shit you have jammed through

your dick and you still knocked her up?" My answering growl is enough to have Coop shut his mouth and hold his hands up. "Just asking, dude. I thought Dee was full of shit when she mentioned all that party you are rocking in your pants." He laughs and wags his brows at me.

"You really need to learn how to shut up. Or maybe buy a filter," Beck says in a loud whisper.

"What? Can you honestly tell me you aren't the least bit interested in why he has all that going on?"

Beck just shakes his head at Coop, choosing to ignore his ridiculous question.

Smart man.

"For the record, I don't make it a habit of thinking about his dick at all." Axel laughs, sitting in one of the chairs next to my desk and picking up a stress ball. "But while we're on the topic, what in the hell compelled you to do that shit?"

"Are we really going to do this? Should we whip them out and compare sizes while we're at it?" I run my hand through my hair in frustration. Ever since word of my piercings got out, I've had a feeling that this would be coming.

Maddox finally chimes in, a wicked grin forming. "No need for that! I know mine trumps all you little boys."

"Wanna bet?" Coop mocks and stands, making to unzip his pants.

"If you pull that shit out in my office, I will cut you."

He wisely sits back down when I reach for my scissors.

"All right. If you really need to know, I lost a bet. An old friend of mine bet me I wouldn't do it, then stepped up the bet that I wouldn't get more than him. So I got wasted, and the rest is history. Melissa loves them, so all in all it's the best bet I ever lost. The end."

They all just look at me. Maddox is the first to break the silence. "You guys should take notes. As funny as you think it is, the ladies love it. Congrats on the baby, brother." And with that, he leaves the room.

I get a few more mumbled congratulations before Beck and Coop get up and leave. Axel never moves from his seat, still just throwing that damn ball up in the air.

"What? I can tell you have something to say." I lean back and get ready to hear him out.

"Did you really have to put ideas in Izzy's head? She now has some brilliant idea that I need some... What did she call it? Oh yeah, 'Trifecta of vaginal bliss.' What in the hell does that shit mean?"

I throw my head back and laugh so hard my sides cramp up. "Do those women tell each other everything?"

"Apparently so. And, Greg, I don't want to hear about your dick anymore."

We talk for a while before he gets serious again.

"I'm happy for you. For all three of you. I know you, and I know this wasn't ever even on your radar. But, brother, this looks good on you."

And just like that, my heart feels full to capacity, my skin feels tight, and that damn smile that's so big it hurts comes rushing back to the surface.

"Thanks, man. Thanks."

I may not have ever dreamt of this life for myself, but I finally feel like I have everything. There isn't anything that can take this feeling from us.

CHAPTER 2

Greg

SIX MONTHS LATER

"**D**ADDDDY!"

Ah. And now the fun begins.

I left Cohen sitting on my bed, harmlessly watching some ridiculous cartoon so that I could jump in the shower. We're running late, but that's pretty typical when Melissa leaves us to our own devices. What does she expect? The 'bad guys' won't kill themselves, blanket forts can't be constructed in a split second, and Lego fortresses won't build themselves. My boy needs to have some one-on-one time with his dad, and with the twins fast approaching we're squeezing in every second of 'man time' that we can.

I smile, drying off as quickly as possible before grabbing my boxer briefs. The last time I made the mistake of forgetting to grab some before I jumped in the shower, I swear Cohen spent an hour talking about wiener-rings after that. Melissa thinks it's hilarious, but I keep envisioning my little dude going to school and announcing to his class that he wants to have earrings in his wiener because his daddy does. That shouldn't make pick-up awkward.

"Daddy, Daddy, DADDY!"

When I step out of the bathroom the first thing I see is Cohen jumping on the bed, his little arms flapping wildly and his ever-present cape flying behind him. With a smile, I hook his little body around the waist with my arm and toss him in the air. Pretty soon he's not going to be small enough for me to toss around, and just the thought of him growing up too quickly makes my chest tighten.

"What's up, little dude?"

His tiny hands cup my face, pulling me closer until our noses touch. "Daddy," he whispers.

I bring my hands up and frame his head, rubbing our noses slightly. "Cohen," I whisper back.

He giggles, his smile growing larger. "Mommy has a funny belly now."

"Yes, little man, she sure does. But, Mommy has your sisters in her funny belly, and pretty soon they're going to be here and she won't have that belly anymore."

His brows crinkle for a second while he processes this. It doesn't take long before he asks the question I've known was coming.

"Daddy?"

"Cohen?"

"How is mommy going to get my babies out of her funny bel-

11

ly?"

Shit. This isn't something Melissa covered.

"Uh…"

His face loses all traces of confusion and his crooked little smile takes its place.

"You don't know! I'm going to ask Dilbert! Dilbert knows everything, Daddy!"

Damn, Sway! There's no way in hell I'm going to let Sway— also referred to by his given name, Dilbert, by only Cohen—give my son sex-ed. I can picture it now. Sway would have Cohen out of his cape and into a wig and heels in no time.

"Come here, son." I take a seat on the bed and hold my arms out, waiting for Cohen to crawl into my lap. His little knees almost take out my dick a few times, and I'm pretty sure I've lost my nuts. He finally settles, sitting on his shins with his knees pressed painfully into my thighs and his tiny hands holding on to my shoulders. "All right, little man. When Mommy has your sisters, the doctor is going to give her a shot so she doesn't feel anything. Then she's going to lie down, and the doctor will carefully take your sisters out. It's all big doctor secrets, and no one will tell Daddy. They even put up a special blue wall that makes it invisible."

With every word I speak, his mocha-colored eyes grow larger and larger. His mouth is hanging open, and the look on his face is nothing short of amazed. Yeah, I know Cohen, and there isn't anything he loves more than a big mystery.

"You with me, C-Man?" I laugh, tickling his sides.

He giggles, jumps down with a large chant of excitement, and takes off to find the magical invisible wall.

"Cohen, get your shoes on! I promised your mommy we

wouldn't be late." I can hear him banging around the house, hopefully on the way to his shoes.

IT TAKES Cohen and me forever, as usual, to get out of the house. He couldn't find his sneakers, so my kid is rocking his red cape, jeans, a tee, and bright orange rain boots. It hasn't rained in Georgia in what feels like years, but Cohen's wearing those damn boots with pride. When we walk into the restaurant where we're meeting everyone, my eyes immediately take in my beautiful wife so that I don't miss a second of her reaction to our boy's outfit.

As she's mid-sentence with Asher, her eyes grow as wide as her beautiful belly, and her hand shoots up to cover her mouth. I can clearly see the laughter shining bright in her eyes from across the dimly lit room. It's not abnormal for Cohen to end up looking like a misfit when I'm in charge of getting him ready. At least it's better than last weekend's bathing suit, tank top that said 'my uncle is cooler than yours'—thank you, Maddox—his cape, and a damn sombrero.

Cohen takes off the second he spots Nate, Axel and Izzy's son, sitting at the end of the table next to his mother. Even with almost two years between those two, they are thick as thieves. I laugh when Cohen immediately starts flailing his arms around and moving around in the wild movements he's so fond of. Nate lets out a laugh so loud that a few diners around the table look over with smiles.

I greet the table, getting friendly welcomes from the ladies in the group and the normal chin lifts and grunts from the guys.

I walk over to Melissa, gently pull her into my arms, and hold her close. I can feel my girls rolling around in her belly when she presses closer.

"Hey, you," she says, her lips a breath away from mine, just begging for me to close the distance.

"Hey back." I pull her close and savor the taste of her on my tongue. I feel her lips tip up, and her moan tingles against my lips. Yeah, my girl missed me today.

"Maybe, just a wild guess here, but maybe those two will remember we aren't in their bedroom, the porn music isn't playing on a loop, and it probably isn't the wisest move to start molesting each other in the family restaurant?"

I break away from Melissa's lips, licking my own when I see the fire burning bright in her eyes.

"Shut up, Ash," I growl and give my wife one more chaste kiss before helping her take her seat again.

"'Shut up, Ash,' he says. No, '*thank you,* Ash, for reminding me that I can't drive the boat into the canal in the middle of family dinner'?"

It takes me a second. For one, I can't stop looking at him as if he's lost his damn mind, but mainly he sounds so much like Coop right now that I have to remind myself who is speaking to me.

"HA! You just called his…hotdog a boat!" Dee starts laughing so hard she's bent over, banging the table with her fist.

Beck just shakes his head with a smile, looking at his fiancée's actions.

"I bet it's more like a tugboat!" Izzy chimes in, gaining Axel's and Chelcie's laughter.

"Seriously? A tugboat?" I should have known better than to let them get the best of me, but really, my pride wouldn't let me sit there with them calling my dick a tugboat. Melissa's hand rubs my leg, trying to keep me from giving these fools what they want.

"No, no…you're right. I was too generous with the boat analogy. I'm sure you're still paddling around with something more like a canoe, right?" Ash smirks before taking a big gulp of his beer.

"Fucking canoe," I grumble under my breath.

"Canoe might be giving him a little too much. Don't they make starter kayaks? Nice and short. Not much girth to those suckers!" I gape at Dee, only making her laugh louder.

Melissa laughs under her breath. "Don't."

"Are we really sitting around, discussing the size of my wiener?"

Melissa's eyes get as large as saucers before she covers her mouth with her hand and bursts out laughing. It takes me a second to figure out why the hell she's joining in with a table full of laughter at me calling my dick a wiener because I'm too busy looking at her belly bouncing with each giggle that escapes.

"Daddy! You said wiener!" My head shoots over to Cohen, who is currently standing in his chair and pointing at me with a big smile on his face.

I'm pretty sure that every single person in the restaurant is looking over at us now. The whole situation gets even more ridiculous when two-year-old Nate starts banging his sippy cup on the table, chanting, "Wiener, wiener, wiener!" over and over.

"Jesus Christ, kill me now." I cross my arms over my chest and wait for everyone to stop laughing so we can get this dinner over with and I can take my wife home.

Melissa leans over, kisses my cheek and whispers in my ear, "I love you—and your tugboat."

Turning my head before she can lean back in her seat, I frame her face in my hands and bring her lips back to mine in a kiss hot enough to burn the building down. Pulling back, I look into her dazed eyes, let a smile full of wicked promise take over, and growl when her face goes soft and her eyes shine bright.

"I'll remind you tonight just what kind of machine I've got between my legs, Beauty."

Her cheeks flame, she closes her eyes on a moan, and right before she turns back to the table, I hear her mutter, "Beast" under her breath.

We've been lucky with her pregnancy so far. According to her doctor, we can continue our sex life—just a little more carefully. Thank Christ. I'm not sure I could last seeing her like this and not be able to sink deep inside her body.

The rest of the dinner passes by with more laughter—not at my expense—loud conversation, and a whole lot of love. These are the moments with my family and friends that I remember just how blessed I am.

I look around the table, feeling a pang in my heart from knowing that we're missing some important people. After we lost Coop, we decided there wouldn't be a week that passed without having a family dinner at least once. It wasn't easy at first. The first few months, Asher was more or less a ghost, sitting there and drinking his dinner in whatever he could grab. He's come a long way, but I can still see the fire to avenge his brother burning deep within him.

Maddox has been to a few here and there, but he's made it clear that until he can get Emmy back home he won't be around. It's been about two weeks since he took off after her, and last I heard, things weren't going well. Having both of them gone has left a large void in our group.

And of course I can't forget Sway, who is usually always at our family dinners. Tonight he's taking Davey out on their first date, and he explained, with way too much detail, why he wouldn't be joining us tonight.

Looking around the table again, catching Axel's and Beck's eyes as they make their own sweep of the table, I know that they're thinking the same thing. So much has changed within our tight-knit group over the last few years. Even with the added members in our 'family,' the loss of the ones who aren't here is very much still felt.

I tip my chin at the guys, grabbing my drink and holding it up briefly before taking a long swallow. Even with the parts of this last year that have tried each and every one of us, I can't help but pray that the worst is behind us. I'm not sure if this group can handle another loss.

Melissa's soft laughter brings me back from my thoughts and I look over to see her smiling at Asher. Of course, the playboy has his charms on bright tonight. He needs a shock collar to remind him not to flirt with my woman.

I throw my arm around the back of her chair and pull her closer to my side, leveling Asher with my darkest look before speaking, "Mine."

He throws his head back and laughs, drawing more attention

from the surrounding tables. "Got it, Fido. Would you like to piss all over her now too?"

"Calm down, you beast." Melissa laughs.

"Calm down? Melissa, I hate to break it to you, but I don't think he's ever going to calm down when it comes to you." I look over at Izzy, smiling my thanks for her rational thinking.

"I know. Isn't it adorable?"

My head shoots back to Melissa. *Adorable?* Puppies are adorable. Babies are adorable... I am not adorable.

Bringing my lips to her ear, I lick and pull her lobe in my mouth before whispering softly and reminding her just how much my adorable tugboat can't wait to get her home, naked, and screaming in pleasure.

Fucking adorable.

CHAPTER 3

Greg

"**D**EEPER... HARDER, please."

I pull back slowly, feeling her walls clamp down on my dick before pushing forward again. Not as hard as she wants, but deep enough that I can feel her womb kiss the tip of my dick.

Looking down at my dick as it slowly pushes in and out of Melissa's soaked pussy has my balls drawing in tight, begging for release.

"Please, Greg, I need it deeper." I ignore her begging, continuing my slow and torturous ministrations. God, I love the feeling of her walls hugging my dick. Feeling her body take mine is the most incredible sensation in the world. Having her slick walls clamp down when she's as close as she is right now, the wetness from her arousal coating both of us... Yeah, it doesn't get any better than this.

With one more push, I bury myself to the root, rolling my hips and groaning when I feel a surge of wetness. She's close. I could end this right now. I'm that close to finding my own release, but I want to make her scream again before I take mine.

I move my hands, which were tightly holding her hips, and run them up her spine. The feeling of her silky smooth skin under my fingertips has me rocking my hips, grinding against her body. I'll never get enough of this woman. My hands finish their journey when I reach her shoulders, curling my fingers, letting her know that I want her to come up off her elbows.

We don't need words anymore. Our bodies know each other so well that all it takes is a few touches, and the rest follows. She comes up on her knees, bringing her arm over her head and grabbing the back of my neck to bring my mouth to hers. Our kiss is nothing short of brutally crazed. Our tongues and teeth nip and lick in a fierce battle of control. Our tongues duel in a dance that sends tingles straight down my spine and wraps a claw-like vise around my balls.

I bring one arm around her chest, palming one perfectly full breast and tweaking her tight nipple with my thumb. My other arm snakes around her middle, caressing her belly lovingly before trailing down her tight skin until I hit her slick heat and her wetness leaks around my fingertips. Giving her a few quick thrusts, I feel myself glide into her welcoming body effortlessly, causing a growl to rumble from deep within my throat.

"Nothing feels better than your pussy soaking my dick."

She moans against my lips, whimpering when I pull out again. "Please, baby, take me harder."

"No." I know what she wants, and I also know that it's killing her not to try and take control. I put the brakes on our rough lovemaking almost two months ago. I don't care what the doctors say.

There is no damn way I'm going to chance taking her too roughly and hurting my girls. No. Won't happen. It's been the only sore spot between us the last few weeks. Melissa wants it hard, and I won't... I can't give that to her.

"Greg..." She tries to push back, but my arms hold her firm.

"Hush, Beauty, and let me love you."

I continue to love her, pushing in with an achingly slow pace before pulling out almost to the point of falling free from her body before repeating the process. I know that she's enjoying it. I can feel the proof running down my shaft. Her moans don't lie. She might crave a rough roll in the sheets, but as long as I can make her scream, I'm still doing it right.

"Greg...killing me... Need you...hard." She gasps between thrusts, her cunt gripping me tight with each begged word that crosses her lips, testing my patience like none other.

"No."

The rumble of her protest vibrating against my chest is the only warning I get before she stuns me to my ass. Literally.

She pushes back hard, her ass hitting my hips and my dick falling from her warm body. In a move that shouldn't look that easy for a seven-months-pregnant woman—with twins, no less—she has her body turned around and her small hands pushing against my chest until I fall to my back. Right there in the middle of our king-sized bed, I watch as my woman comes to life above me.

We've been as conservative as it gets the last month or so of her pregnancy. The bigger the girls get, the harder almost every position gets. It's pretty much down to me taking her from behind, standing beside the bed so that I don't crush the girls, or lying there while she rides me the best she can with the weight of her belly throwing her off balance. You won't hear me complain. I'll take it however she wants to give it to me. Except for the one way she's been begging to for the last three weeks.

My girl wants me to fuck her brains out. No more of this slow and torturous lovemaking. Not for Melissa. No, she wants me to fuck her raw, and it scares the shit out of me.

"I'm sick of you treating me like I'm spun from glass. News flash, Greg Cage—I'm not going to break. Your massive dick isn't going to thump a baby on the head, scar her for life, or poke a hole in her head. But what your dick is going to do is get the hell inside me and fuck me hard!"

I stare up at her as she climbs onto my body. Her face flushed, tits full and swaying with her movements, and her gorgeous body ripe with pregnancy, as she moves over my throbbing dick and impales herself roughly. She throws her head back, her hands going to my thighs and her pussy clenching and rippling around my straining erection.

"Shit…" I hiss, my hands shooting to her hips to help steady her movements. She doesn't even notice me, her body using mine for everything she's been craving.

I watch, fighting my body to not come instantly as she lets loose and takes what she wants. Her body rides me with ease. With each downward grind, she rolls her hips, and I feel her walls quiver. It doesn't take long before I can feel her cream leaking out and running down my balls, her movements becoming choppier. Her breathing speeds up and her rhythm falters. I quickly take over so that she doesn't overdo it.

Holding her hips steady, I begin pumping my hips with the powerful thrusts she's been begging for. Her arms shoot forward, bracing her weight against my chest when she can no longer hold herself up without help. Her fingers curl, and her nails break the skin, instantly my balls start to pull tight at the blinding pleasure her pain causes.

"Give it to me. Let me feel you suck my dick deep with your tight pussy. Come on... Give it to me, Beauty."

She sucks in a shallow breath, her eyes locking with mine for a second before she throws her head back and screams her pleasure. I pull her against my dick, her wetness soaking me as I erupt deep within her tight body.

I move us so that we're both lying on our sides, my dick still hard and hugged by her body, and enjoy the way she comes back from a hard orgasm. Her glossy eyes struggle to focus, her mouth is open slightly, and her tits rub against my body with each deep pull she takes.

"I love you, my Beauty."

She smiles, her hand coming up to my cheek before pressing a kiss to my lips. "And I love you, my Beast."

Knowing that she isn't far from falling asleep, I pull her in tight and enjoy the feeling of her in my arms and her swollen belly pressed against my abdomen. Feeling each roll and kick my girls offer brings a smile to my face. With all my girls in my arms, I fall asleep with a full heart.

CHAPTER 4

Melissa

SHIT.

I'm going to piss myself if I can't figure out how to get out of Greg's arms soon. He sleeps like this every night, with my body pulled tight to his and my back against his chest. His arm is around my belly, and his palm is holding firm against the girls. Even in his sleep, he's protecting us. I would smile and think about how it's the sweetest, most loving gesture ever if his heavy-ass arm wasn't pressing against my body in a way that has my bladder, which is already fighting for prime real estate, threatening to burst.

Yeah, this would all be the best in the world—if I weren't about to wet the bed.

Maybe I need some Depends? God, soon I'm going to be walking around in adult diapers with the way the girls are growing. I'm not sure there's much more room left for them to grow! Greg loves my pregnant belly, and I bet if he had his way, he would keep me pregnant year round. As much as I love being pregnant, I'm ready for this to be over.

Unfortunately for me, there isn't an end in sight for at least another two months. Even with as uncomfortable as I am, and as much as I wish I knew what my damn pussy looked like, I'm happy to bake my little princesses for as long as I can.

"Greg, wake up, baby. I need to pee."

He doesn't move. His arm doesn't let up.

"Greg, please. I need to go."

Squeezing my legs together, praying that I can hold it, I try and wiggle free with no luck. His arms pull me closer and my already screaming bladder starts blaring the warning alarm.

"Oh, God." I try moving his arm again, but he grumbles something about tugboats and yachts before pulling me even closer. "Shit."

This isn't going to be pretty if I can't get up in the next minute. I try to wake him up gently a few times with no luck. Finally, left with no other option, I pull my arm up before bringing my elbow down, driving it back into his gut. He jumps up with a shout, his feet tangling with the sheets before he falls flat on his ass over the side of the bed. I don't even have time to enjoy the hilarity of the situation before I'm over the edge and wobbling to the bathroom in a sprint that I'm sure makes me look like a penguin running a marathon.

I close my eyes and moan with the pleasure of an empty bladder. I lean back against the toilet and rub my belly while I finish my business. When I finally finish and open my eyes, I see that I've gained an audience.

"You couldn't try a simple wake-up, babe?"

I cock my brow, ignoring him while I finish up in the bathroom. He just stands there, no shame in his mouthwatering nakedness, rubbing his stomach while his eyes take in every inch of my body.

"God, you look good enough to eat."

I laugh, washing my hands before turning around and closing the distance between us. "You're impossible. The next time I spend ten minutes attempting to wake your ass up while you try to hold my body captive, I'm just going to piss all over you." I smile sweetly at him, laughing when his eyes widen.

"I love it when you talk dirty to me, wife." He smiles down at me, pulling me closer before lowering his mouth to mine. Our kiss is slow and teasing. I can feel his length hardening against my belly, my hands wrapping around his body before gripping his firm ass in my hands and squeezing him closer. He doesn't waste a second before pulling me back to the bed and showing me how good slow and lazy lovemaking can be.

Twice.

By the time we finally fall asleep, the sun is starting to peek through the blinds, and I thank my stars that Dee and Beck took Cohen home with them last night.

I fall asleep with a smile on my face and my husband's arms wrapped tightly around his girls again.

Only to wake up ten minutes later, fighting free of his hold before I wet the bed…again.

"WHAT'S YOUR plan for today?" I ask Greg when he walks into the kitchen later that morning. His worn jeans are hugging his ass perfectly, and his arms stretching the limits of the University of Georgia football tee he's wearing. I'm half tempted to drag him back to bed.

"Figured I would run over to grab Cohen, but Beck just called and said they wanted to take him to the aquarium today and they would have him home before dinner. You're stuck with me, woman." He bends down and gives me a quick kiss before walking over to the coffee maker.

"Good. You have a full day of putting the girls' cribs together then." I beam up at him when he groans. We've been putting off the assembly of the girls' cribs for a few weeks now. Greg took one look at all the "damn little pieces" and put it aside for another day.

"And I don't suppose you plan on helping with this adventure?"

"Nope. I have a full day at the spa. Remember, Sway gave it to me for a baby shower gift? All the girls—well, and Sway—are coming. I'll be gone all day, at least."

"Spa?" He folds his thick arms across his chest, and my mouth waters from watching his shirt stretch tight against his arms.

"Uh…yeah." I clear my throat, looking up into his knowing eyes. "Manicures, pedicures, a pregnancy massage… The normal spa type stuff."

"Massage?" The edge to his voice clues me in to just where his mind has drifted.

"You don't need to go all caveman on me, Greg. It's perfectly fine for pregnant women to get massages. No one is going to touch me like you're thinking."

"If you want a massage then we can go back upstairs and I'll give you one."

"I love you, but I'm going, and I'm going to enjoy the hell out of Lars rubbing my stiff muscles." I shouldn't joke, but he really makes it too easy.

"Fucking Lars." He takes two powerful steps towards me before gently pulling me up from my chair. "Fucking *Lars* better not touch any part of your body. *Lars* better go ahead and go to another state while you're inside that spa. No way in hell do I want *Lars* anywhere near your body. This is *my* body, Melissa. If anyone is going to rub your stiff muscles, it will be *me*." His deep voice grinds out the words, causing my panties to flood with my wetness and my pussy to clench. I shouldn't provoke him, but hell, this is so hot.

"But, Greg, they say his hands are magic." I bite the inside of my cheek to keep from laughing when his growl rumbles around me. His blue eyes darken to the navy color I love, the color that means my beast isn't far from the surface. I've got him right where I want him. My pregnancy hormones are making me almost ravenous with my sex drive.

"I'll show you magic." I yelp when he clears the table with one swipe of his arm. He drops down to his knees and makes quick work of my jeans. Luckily, another plus of maternity clothes—those elastic waistbands. Before I even have time to take a breath, my bare ass is propped up on the edge of the table and my husband's mouth is feasting between my thighs.

He doesn't waste a second. His lips suck and lick every inch of my pussy but ignore the only spot I want his mouth to be. I don't even recognize the sounds coming from my mouth, while I'm holding my body up with one arm behind me and the other is holding his head against me as I ride his mouth. The second he brings his fingers into the mix, finger-fucking me to one mind-blowing orgasm after the next, I'm screaming the walls down.

I didn't even feel him stop, my body still coming down from the power of my release, but when I feel the cool steel of his Prince Albert against my opening, my eyes open and lazily drink him in. His jeans are pushed down to his knees, and his long, thick cock is ready to plunge into my body. His eyes are hooded, alight with desire.

I bring my hand between us, wrapping my fist as far as I can around his velvet skin, and help him guide himself into my wet heat. There isn't anything sweet and slow about our coming together. He finally takes me how I've been begging him to take me. His balls smack against my ass, and his fingers dig into my hips when he drags me closer to the edge of the table. I can hear how wet I am when he thrusts into my body, the sound intensifying the feelings that are racing through my veins.

When he brings his thumb and presses against my clit, I shoot off in another orgasm so powerful that my hand slips out from behind me and I almost fall to the table. He grunts and pauses in his thrusting to help me keep my balance before powering into my body, the new angle causing each one of the three piercings I love so much to hit all the right spots. I throw my head back and come all over him.

I hear him moaning and grunting before I feel his release bathe my walls.

After a few minutes, both of our breathing returns to normal and I look up at his smug grin.

"How's that for magic?"

And that's why I love poking the beast.

CHAPTER 5

Greg

MELISSA HAS been gone for a few hours now, and I'm still struggling to put the twins' cribs together. You would think that something as simple as a bed for a baby wouldn't be so complicated, but damn.

Throwing the directions that, of course, are only in German, I jog down to the kitchen to grab a beer. Propping my ass against the counter, I get lost in my thoughts, remembering when Melissa and I found out we were about to have two little ones and not just one.

There are moments in your life when you know that a higher power is at work. That someone is hard at work making sure that all the bad you've ever felt in your life is cashed in for something so incredibly perfect it almost doesn't seem real.

For me, just finding out that Melissa was carrying my child is a moment I will never forget. We had become a family the day we officially adopted Cohen, and even though I love that boy as if he were my own, there's something to be said about creating a life with the woman you love. Knowing that Cohen is just as excited as we are is just icing on the cake.

Complete. This is what it must feel like to own the whole world.

"Greg? Are you even listening to a thing I'm saying?" Melissa laughs from the passenger seat.

I look over and smile when I see her stomach. I would never tell her this, but I swear she grew again overnight. She started showing early and never really slowed down. At almost four months, I swear she looks further along. Her doctor explained that this was just because she is so small to begin with. Every day, her body changes more, and it's sexy as hell to watch.

"Greg?" she prompts.

"Sorry. Just thinking."

"Well, if that goofy grin is anything to go by, it's nothing about our baby and more about your insatiable hormones." She laughs and rubs her belly some more.

Reaching over I place my hand right above hers and drum my fingers softly. "Are you excited?" I ask, rubbing her stomach a few times before taking her hand in mine and lacing our fingers together. When she told me that we could find out what we're having before her twenty-week appointment, I jumped all over that.

"God, yes! I can't wait to find out if we're having a boy or a girl. Cohen told me this morning on the way to daycare that he thinks he's having a sister."

This has been an ongoing discussion. Cohen and I both think it's a girl, but Melissa thinks it's a boy. I couldn't care less as long as our baby is healthy.

"You still going with the whole 'there is no way I would be this

big if it isn't a boy' argument?" Her line of reasoning even sounds ridiculous to me, but hey, I'm not going to argue with her.

She looks over at me with a big smile. "Seriously, look at you, Greg! You're huge. There is no way this is a girl. I bet you our son comes out with little baby muscles."

"Baby muscles? Maybe we just have a really healthy baby," I laugh. "You should just admit that your men know everything now and save you the let-down when the doctor confirms it."

She smacks me on the arm and laughs. We continue to the doctor's office in a comfortable silence, holding hands and enjoying the moment.

Pure happiness.

Once we get all checked in and back into the dimly lit room for the ultrasound, I start to get a little nervous. Even though I can tell my girl is pregnant, it still feels so much more real when I look at the monitor and see the life we created. Every one of her appointments has made me feel this way.

The first time I heard our baby's heartbeat, I thought I was going to turn into a blubbering fool. When we got our first ultrasound picture confirming the pregnancy, I felt like I was having a heart attack. There really is no way to explain the overwhelming love I feel for this baby and Melissa.

"Ah, good morning, Cage family!" Melissa's doctor comes in and starts asking her all the routine questions before measuring her stomach and pushing it all over the place. I hate this part. Melissa grabs my hand and just smiles up at me, reminding me that the doctor isn't hurting her.

"Will we be able to determine the gender today, Dr. Nicholson?" Melissa asks softly.

I squeeze her hand out of reflex. We've both been looking forward to this since the day she told me she was pregnant, but more importantly, we have a little dude at home anxiously awaiting the news on his new sibling.

"Yes, Melissa dear. Sixteen weeks on the dot, perfect gestational age to take a look and see." He smiles down at her, his weathered face clearly happy to be a part of this. I swear this man is never in a bad mood. "Are you ready, son? This is a big day for you, too."

"Yes, sir. We can't wait."

He smiles and pats me on the back before getting Melissa ready for her ultrasound.

When he places the wand on her bump and starts spreading the gel around, I look up at his face. I don't know why I was focusing on him and not the monitor, but I notice immediately when his bushy white brows pull together and his lips purse in thought. I immediately get worried. I know that Melissa senses that something is off because she's looking at his face too.

"Doc?" I question, not even ashamed of the slight quiver that gives my fear away.

"What? Oh...yes, everything is okay. Just wasn't expecting... that." he says softly. Almost as if he's questioning himself.

"Doc, I don't mean any disrespect here, but you're kind of freaking us out." Melissa whimpers softly, and I know that she's barely holding it in. I lean down and lightly kiss her before turning my attention back to Dr. Nicholson.

"I'm sorry, Melissa, Greg... I was just making sure..." He trails off and turns the monitor towards us before placing the wand back on her stomach. "All right, you see here? This is the first

head, and you see here? This is the second. Quite tricky. You have a little hider!" He laughs.

Melissa hasn't said anything. She's just looking at the doctor in complete shock.

"What the hell? My baby has two heads!?" I practically scream. Why is everyone so calm? My baby is going to be born with two heads!

My outburst seems to clear Melissa of her fog. Before I can get another word out, she reaches up and smacks the side of my head.

"Seriously, Greg?" She laughs, joining the already laughing doctor.

What the hell is so funny? Aren't they at all worried about my two-headed baby?

"Oh dear, I'm very sorry. I should have been more clear, Greg. This," he says, pointing at the monitor again, "is Baby A's head, and this one is Baby B's. Congratulations. It appears as if you are having twins, and sneaky ones at that. Hiding this whole time. And... Oh yes, very clear. Do you two want to know the genders?" He looks at Melissa first, who I assume nods her head. I'm still stuck back at my two-headed baby.

No, not two heads.

Twins.

"Holy shit. We're having twins?" I whisper, looking down at Melissa. She's smiling her beautiful, blinding smile at me. Tears slowly roll down her cheeks. "Beauty, we're having twins!"

She laughs as I cover her mouth in a passionate kiss. After a few seconds, she pushes me back, reminding me where we are. When I look up at Dr. Nicholson, he's just smiling at the monitor.

"Please, we would like to know."

"I figured as much. Quite a shock, but a happy one. And now that they have decided to let us know their little secret, they aren't being shy at all." He pulls the wand away and turns to us with a smile. "Congratulations again. Your twin daughters look perfectly healthy." He continues to talk to Melissa while I stare at the picture in my hand of my babies.

Twins!

I don't let her hand go once on the way to pick up Cohen. When we pull up at his daycare, I run in with a big smile on my face.

"Daddy!" Before I even have the door to his classroom open completely, his small body is barreling towards me. "Daddy, did you see it? Was I right? Is it a girl? Does it have a wiener? What is Mommy going to do if it has a wiener? She can't look at them. Did you see it?"

I laugh and pull him up into my arms. "Well, hello to you too, C-Man."

"Hi, Daddy. Do I have a sister? Is she pretty like Mommy? Do you think she can fight ninjas?" When I don't answer, his small hands grab my cheeks and pull my face towards his. Nose to nose, smile to smile. God, I love this kid. "Was I right?" he asks with all the seriousness a four-year-old can muster.

"Can't tell you yet. You know that wouldn't be fair to Mommy. She wants to see your handsome face when we tell you the news." I kiss his nose and continue out the door, waving to the teachers on the way.

"I know I'm right, Daddy, but I'll still be happy for Mommy so she thinks she got a secret." He snickers a few times before waving at Melissa from across the parking lot.

Cohen continues his questions during the whole fifteen-minute ride home. I think I've heard the word wiener more times than I knew possible to fit into one conversation. Melissa just continues to smile at him and holds off his questions.

By the time we pull up at the house, he is bouncing in his seat. The second the car shuts off, he takes off running around the drive-way. I help Melissa out, and we make our way inside, Cohen still asking a million questions behind us.

"Cohen, baby, calm down." Melissa laughs, pulling him closer.

"Can't!" he screams with a big smile. "I gotta know! Was I right? Am I going to have a sister? I have to know so I can practice. I gotta protect my sister!"

I sit down next to Melissa and pull him into my lap. "All right, buddy. You know how we got to use that special camera today to see inside Mommy's belly? Well, we found out something else today. The doctor said that there isn't just one, but two babies in there, and you were right. You are getting a sister, only now you're getting two sisters."

"What? How did the other sister get in there? Is she magic? Do I have a magic sister?"

I can feel Melissa's body shaking with silent laughter, and I know there will be no help from her here. "Uh, well...the doctor said she was playing hide and seek."

Cohen starts smiling and nods his head. "This is good, Daddy. I knew my angels would give me sisters. I asked them."

Melissa stops laughing and grabs my hand. "What do you mean, baby?" she asks on a whisper.

"I asked Nana, Mommy Fia, and Auntie Grace to give me a sister. I said I wanted a sister more than anything in the world so I

can look out for her like Daddy looks out for you."

"Oh, Cohen. You're such a special little man." she says, kissing his cheek.

"I know what I want to name my sisters." he says, clearly proud of himself for his prediction and making Melissa happy.

"All right, let's hear it." I lean back, intertwine my fingers with Melissa's, and wait. I don't realize I am holding my breath until his soft voice speaks the names.

"I want my sisters to have my angel's names. Lillian Sofia for Nana and Mommy Fia, and Lyndsie Grace for Daddy's mommy and Auntie Grace."

My breath comes out in a rush, and I can feel Melissa breathing heavily next to me. Cohen just looks at us with his little smile and bright eyes, waiting for the moment when we confirm that he's allowed to name his sisters.

"Lillian Sofia and Lyndsie Grace? Cohen, I think those are perfect names for your sisters. You're already such a wonderful big brother." she whispers.

He gives us a big hug before leaping off my lap and running through the house. We can hear him talking to his 'angels,' telling them about his new sisters. I pull Melissa closer, resting my lips against her temple and my hand against her stomach. With all my girls in my arms and a full heart, I enjoy the moment of life coming full circle.

It's times like this that I remember just how far I've come in the last few years. After losing my sister, I questioned my path in life. I questioned every single relationship I had. I wondered if having other people in my life was worth the pain if I was going to lose them. It wasn't until Melissa and Cohen came into my life, that I realized living in fear is almost the same as slowly dying.

From the day I met her, I knew I would fight every day to be the man worthy of her love.

Hearing my cell ringing from another room, I shake off my daydreams and follow the sound.

I let out a relieved breath when I see Axel's name across the screen.

"What are you doing?" No sense wasting time. If I don't have these cribs together when Melissa gets home, there will be hell to pay.

"Well, I was enjoying breakfast in bed, but when your ass wouldn't stop calling, Izzy made me stop. So, thanks for that, jack-ass."

"Ha, yeah…sorry about that, but welcome to my world. Just wait until Nate is a master at cockblocking like Cohen. I swear, when that boy is home, he has some sort of sensor that goes off when I'm about to enjoy Melissa."

"He's already started. Last night, just sunk into Iz and he's screaming about turtles. Do you have any idea what a two-year-old screaming about turtles will do to your sex life? Iz started laughing so hard that my dick got the message loud and clear." He lets out a breath full of frustration, and the smile on my face grows. Yeah, sounds like a normal day in the Cage house.

"As much fun as this little chat is, I need you to come over and help me get these damn cribs together. I hold one end up, but then the second I go to attach something, the damn thing falls on my head. If I want to enjoy my wife tonight, I have to get this shit done."

"Yeah? Poor guy." He starts laughing; I'm sure he's picturing me in a mess of crib parts.

I let a laugh out remembering how the last bang on the head must have looked. "Laugh all you want. The directions are in German, Ax. Luckily I can read the damn things, but it's been a few years, and my German is rusty at best. It's a shame Maddox isn't here. Damn fool would have this shit done by now," I bait, knowing Axel won't be able to resist the challenge of being better than Maddox.

"The hell with that. I'm on the way. Be there in ten."

I laugh, throwing the phone down when I hear him disconnect in my ear.

Maybe if I'm lucky, he'll do all the hard work and I can sit back and enjoy a beer.

CHAPTER 6

Melissa

EXHAUSTED.

That is the only way I can explain what I feel like being halfway through my seventh month of pregnancy. Don't get me wrong; I love *almost* everything about being pregnant. Even the stuff I don't love about carrying around an extra forty—cough, fifty—pounds of baby still brings a smile to my face every time I feel one of my girls kick my kidney, squeeze my bladder, or stick a head in my ribs.

Yeah, I love carrying around my girls.

The best part, the part that keeps that smile on my face even when I feel as though my body is about to split in two, is knowing that these two little princesses are a product of the love I share with their daddy.

There isn't a single day that goes by that I don't thank God that Greg was set in my path. I was living a life that was half empty, and now, my glass is overflowing.

I finally pull my car into the driveway and smile when I see that the lights are on, flooding the yard with their warmth.

"Daddy isn't going to be happy we've been gone all day, little ladies," I whisper to my belly, running my hand across my hard abdomen, and smile when I feel my girls give some solid kicks.

It takes me longer than normal to pull my body out of the car. I was driving around Greg's truck until it became too hard to get in and out of the cab. I miss driving that monster around, but it was impossible to heave my weight into the driver's seat anymore. I hate this damn car. I feel like I sit so low to the ground that I'll be run over by every vehicle that comes near me. Luckily for me— or unluckily, considering I never pictured myself owning a mini-van—Greg promised we would go car shopping soon.

"Well, well... It looks like my wife decided she still loves her men after all." I smirk when I hear my husband's deep voice coming from behind me. I don't turn; instead, I spend a second relishing in the soothing tones that wash over my tired body, firing alive every single inch. Even with his teasing tone, my body recognizes its mate, causing my skin to pucker with tiny goose bumps.

"Turn around, Beauty."

I visibly shutter when his demand hits my ears. Slowly, I turn and take in all six foot three inches of solid male perfection. His dark brown hair is all over the place, a sure sign that he's been playing with Cohen and running his fingers through his silky locks. I avoid his eyes and let mine travel slowly down his body. A tight black tee hugs every single inch of his chest, arms, and abs. I can literally see each and every muscle outline through the thin cotton. Letting my eyes wander lower, I have to bite my lip when I can see his thick erection straining the front of his sweats, just begging for my touch.

It isn't until I hear his groan that I look up to meet his blazing eyes. The beautiful blue eyes I love so much have darkened to the point that I know he's hanging on by a thread.

My tongue slips past my lips, rolling against my bottom lip before pulling it between my teeth. His eyes flash with warning, and the energy in the garage hits new levels of desire.

"If our boy weren't sitting in the next room, ready to cook his mom dinner, I would have you spread out on the top of that damn car. Fuck. Melissa, baby, you have no idea how much I wish I could sink into your body right now." He crosses the space that separates us, takes my purse from my hands, and lets it fall to the floor before pulling me close. "My cock is begging, baby, weeping to be inside your tight, slick pussy." He lets out a tortured moan before shoving his head into the crook of my neck.

"God, Greg. You can't go all Beast mode on me when you know there isn't anything we can do about it for *hours!* Hours, Greg. My hormones are going insane right now."

"Someone isn't being very patient." I can feel his lips tipping up against my neck before he presses small, hot kisses against my skin. "Does my woman want my dick? Huh? Do you want me to take it slow, letting each one of my piercings rub against you, rub inside of that wet pussy until it hits that spot that always makes you fly through the roof? Hmm?" His lips keep kissing. Tiny, wet, closed-mouth kisses against my shoulder and neck. With each word he speaks, I feel as if my body were being set on fire. My clit is throbbing against my soaked panties. "Or do you want me to take you hard, letting my balls slap against that perfect ass of yours?"

When his hands snake around my body and roughly squeeze

my cheeks, I swear I come. Right then and there, with just his words, I feel the waves of my orgasm crashing over me. His head shoots up and his eyes question, but the cocky smile on his face tells me that he knows exactly what his words caused.

"Or maybe we should just pour some tea and *talk?*"

Arrogant jerk.

I playfully smack his chest before I drop my forehead to his chest. Yeah, those pregnancy hormones I mentioned also turn me into a complete basket case. I don't do embarrassed, but with flushed cheeks and desire still racing through my veins, I start bawling. Not cute tears and soft sniffles. No, these are body-shaking, breath-gasping, puffy-face, and snotty-nose emotions.

"Hey, what the hell, baby?" His hands cup my cheeks and bring my head up so that my eyes meet his. "Melissa? What's this all about?"

"I'm... so sor—sorry." I hiccup.

"Why on earth are you apologizing?"

I can tell he's worried. His eyes are almost panicked from trying to figure out what set his crazy, hormonal wife off this time. He pulls me away just far enough so that he can look down my body and check for some visible reason for me to be losing my mind.

"I wah-wah-was hoping yo-you would take me."

His thumbs wipe my tears away, the worried look still very much present. "Take you where, Beauty?"

"Tay-tay-take me... on the car!" I wail. Oh, God. He's going to think I'm some sexy-crazed loon.

With wide eyes, I watch the fear bleed from his face and his cocky smile returns. "You need me, Beauty?" That voice. That full-on Beast-mode voice. That is exactly what makes me go from zero to ready to be taken hard.

"Every second…of every day."

His smile grows at my words, and then his lips press roughly against mine and his arms wrap around my body, pulling me as close as he can without pushing too hard against my belly.

Just like always, he knows how to deliver every promise to come in just one kiss. A kiss that is so powerful and all-consuming that I'm climbing right back up that peak and about to tumble over into another orgasm.

"Ew! Daddy! Mommy is touching your butt!"

I groan against Greg's lips when Cohen's voice comes from the doorway to the house. I pull my lips away, give Greg a heated look, and then step around my husband to wrap my arms around Cohen.

"Shh, C-Man. He had ants in his pants, and I had to make sure I got them all."

He giggles, kisses my cheek, and then presses two kisses against my stomach before running back into the house. "Come on, Mommy! We're having sketty!"

Hours later, I am just coming down from my third orgasm in a row. My body is slick with sweat, and my heart is still racing. My toes may be permanently curled.

"I'm pretty sure I can't move my legs."

Greg laughs from where he is lying—or more like collapsed— next to me. "I'm pretty sure I can't move anything."

I turn to my side to relieve the pressure my growing belly is putting on my back. I look over at his profile. His are eyes closed, hair wet with perspiration, and his chest is still moving rapidly.

"Thank you," I whisper so softly I didn't even think he would be able to hear me.

His eyes open and he turns towards me giving me all of his attention. "For what?"

My cheeks heat briefly before I answer. "For loving me."

"Hey, that is one thing you never need to thank me for. Beauty, do you even have a clue to how much I love you?" He shifts, moving so that he can pull me against his side. I rest my head against his chest while one of his hands wraps around my shoulders, holding me close and his hand resting against my belly. "Melissa, I tell you daily—many times—how much I love you. Knowing that you're my wife, that the perfect little boy asleep down the hall is my son because of you, and these little angels are a gift our love made… Those are just some of the things you have given me that makes my life worth living." He pauses, removing his hand from my stomach long enough to lift my chin up so he can look into my eyes. "You never need to thank me for loving you, Melissa. You make it effortless."

I close my eyes, letting the tears that had been pooling tip over and run down my cheeks.

"God, Baby… Don't cry. There isn't anything in our lives that warrants those tears. As far as I can tell, we're about one step from perfect. Once Lillian and Lyndsie get here, there isn't much of anything that could make our world any better. That is, unless you want to give me more babies."

I smile at his attempt at bringing the crazy hormones back down. "Do you ever worry? Things have been going so well that

I'm almost afraid to believe that it's finally time for us to have our happily ever after." He snorts, and I know that he's thinking about all the books I always have my nose stuck in. "Don't you make fun of me, Greg Cage."

His laughter quiets, and he looks down into my eyes. "There isn't a damn thing in this world that can keep us from our happily ever after," he vows before kissing me sweetly. "Sleep, Beauty. Tomorrow's going to be crazy enough, so you need to rest while you can."

I cuddle as close as I can get, letting the sound of his heartbeats lull me to sleep.

CHAPTER 7

Greg

OF COURSE, the one day I promise Melissa that I won't do anything work related, I get a call from Axel about an issue at the office. A damn 'issue' is the last thing I want to deal with today, especially knowing that it more than likely has to do with Mrs. Hutchins, our newest and most aggravating client.

Mrs. Hutchins first came to us about a month ago, convinced that her older husband was sleeping with every female around. She calls constantly. She stops by the office daily. There isn't a damn thing we can say to convince the woman that her husband is very much faithful. She doesn't believe it. I'm starting to get the impression that she is only comes around because she has her eyes on Asher.

During the first meeting we took with her, she all but offered to pay Axel and me to sleep with her. Even if I weren't the happiest damn married man around, there isn't a check large enough that would convince me to sleep with her. She has something evil scratching the surface, and I want that as far away from me as possible.

If only Asher could see things the same way. I know that he hasn't yet, but he's thinking about it, and I know that if he sinks into that woman, she will leave him with something he can never wash off.

Shaking off the creepy-as-hell feeling Mrs. Hutchins always leaves me with, I jog up the stairs in search of my wife. I can hear her and Cohen's laughter coming out of our bedroom and head that way.

"Why do my angels have a party when they're still in your belly? They can't open any presents when they're in your belly. Do you think we'll get cake? I love cake. Will Dilbert be there?"

I smile, walk over to Melissa, and wrap my arms around to rest against her swollen belly as Cohen continues his random questioning.

He finally stops talking and jumps off the bed. Without even a word, he takes off running out the bedroom door.

Melissa and I both laugh at the tornado that is Cohen Cage. Damn, I love that kid.

"Sometimes I wonder if he just talks because he likes the sound of his voice. You know, almost every time he starts on his twenty questions, they end in him running off without even having one answer."

I laugh because she isn't wrong. But Cohen is a boy full of energy, and if asking a million questions and fighting imaginary villains is what it takes, then hey, I can work with that.

Melissa turns with her smile beaming. I thought I was being careful to mask my expression, but she must have noticed that my mood was off because her smile slips and she looks at me with wide, hopeful eyes.

"Beauty…" I start.

"Don't you Beauty me, Greg. You promised you would make it clear to Axel that you weren't doing anything work related today. It's my baby shower, and while I know this isn't something you have any interest in attending, it means something to me. Everyone is excited. Cohen is through-the-roof excited. And I *was* excited until I realized that you're not going to be there."

She takes a breath, but before she can continue, I interrupt her. "Melissa, if it were any other client, I wouldn't even think about it. I need this woman taken care of *before* our girls get here. Axel can't deal with her alone, Beck can't deal with her at all, and Asher isn't allowed to deal with her. With Maddox gone, it's only me." I lean my forehead against hers and take a deep breath. "She's one of our highest-paying clients, Melissa, and even though we live a comfortable life, I can't help my worries with our girls coming. We're going from a family of three to one of five overnight."

Her face softens and her eyes lose their wounded look. I know she wants me there—hell, I want to be there—but I'm not lying.

"It's that terribly nasty trophy wife, isn't it?"

She may think she has me fooled with that bored tone, but I know she and the other girls secretly plot ways to make Mrs. Hutchins disappear.

"Yeah, Beauty. It's her." I brace for it because I know it's coming.

"I hate that plastic, home-wrecking, troll-trotting, skank bitch," she seethes.

She isn't unjust with her hatred either. Between her, Izzy, and

Dee, each of them has witnessed her attempt at getting their men to stray. We joke about it, because they know we would never even think about it, but when it comes down to it, we all want her out of our lives.

"I know, and you aren't alone. We agreed a few weeks ago that we wouldn't take meetings with her alone anymore. She threw herself at Beck, which is why he flat-out refuses to even be near her. Asher is out of town so he can't help. It's just me, and baby, as much as I hate it, I can't let Axel deal with her alone."

She nods her head in understanding, "I know. I get it, I really do, but that doesn't mean I like it." She hugs me close, and I rest my chin on the top of her head.

"I'll be there before you even open your first gift or play your first game. Promise."

She smiles, though it doesn't quite reach her eyes. "I know you will. Now, go get Cohen dressed, please. No rain boots with shorts though!"

After getting Cohen dressed and waiting until Melissa was finally ready to go, I helped her buckle Cohen into her car before pulling her into my arms and giving her a deep kiss.

"Before the first gift, I'll be there," I remind her, hating that I'm letting her down, even just a little.

"I know," she smiles. "I'm not upset, I just wish you didn't have to go. I love you and everything you do for us. Missing a baby shower really isn't a big deal. I'm sorry I made you feel bad earlier, but my hormones are all over the place." She laughs, and the blush she seemed to adopt when she got pregnant spreads across her cheeks.

"I love you and your crazy hormones."

She smiles and gives me another deep kiss. "I love you, too." Laughing, she folds herself awkwardly behind the wheel.

I make a mental note to go straight to the dealership before the week ends and get her the minivan we've been talking about for a while now.

"BUT, GREG, isn't there something else you can do? I just know that Harry is sleeping with that woman. I saw the way she looked at him. There is no way that a woman who hasn't seen him naked would look at him like that."

"It's Mr. Cage, Mrs. Hutchins, and as Mr. Reid has gone over with you already, there is no evidence that points to any infidelity on your husband's behalf. We've been watching him closely since the day you walked into our office for the *first* time. There hasn't been a single grain of proof that we could even offer to you. I'm positive that this is a good report, correct?"

We've been playing this game for the last thirty minutes. I keep checking my watch, knowing that Melissa should be at the country club that the girls are using to host her shower by now. If I plan on keeping true to my promise, I need to get this woman out of our building as soon as possible.

"Oh, don't be silly, Greg. I told you to call me Alison," she purrs. Literally purrs. Axel rolls his eyes from his perch across the room. He's about to blow, and I'm not far behind him.

"Mrs. Hutchins, how about this? We will put the cameras back up inside your home as well as his office for another two weeks and then reevaluate at the end of that time?"

She instantly brightens when I confirm that we aren't cutting her loose. Shit. Axel's going to flip.

"Darling, that is just perfect." She makes a move to touch my arm and I pull back roughly.

After another five minutes of bullshit, she finally agrees to a time for us to come and reinstall the equipment in her home. Another pain in the ass, but this time I wouldn't make the mistake of showing up alone.

"Swear to Christ, I'm ready to just say to hell with the ridiculous amount of money she's paying us and cut her loose. She's like a fucking parasite."

I laugh at Axel and flip the lock on the front door. "Give her another two weeks of babysitting her monk of a husband and that's it. If I weren't in a rush to get to the baby shower the girls are throwing Melissa, I wouldn't have even given her that."

Axel follows behind as I make my way down the hallway and into my office to grab my keys and the files I need to go over at home tomorrow for the upcoming week.

"You aren't telling me anything I don't know. Izzy almost took off my head when I told her I would be late for the shower," he laughs, palming his keys and following me out the door. "That woman actually offered to 'service' me before you showed up. It's a shame it isn't the husband who hired us. Wouldn't even take five minutes before we had a stack full of proof."

"Pain in the ass. That's all she is. But right now, I couldn't care less," I chuckle, pausing my steps off the sidewalk when my phone starts ringing. My brow pulls tight when Axel's own cell starts ringing too. "Popular, I guess."

He snorts and we both pull our phones out.

"Izzy," he smiles.

Looking down and seeing Dee's name across my screen has my stomach dropping. I can't shake the feeling that something isn't right as I stare at Dee's smiling face on my phone.

I swipe my thumb across the screen to answer, but before I can speak, I notice Axel's look of pure terror as he stands a few feet in front of me with his phone pressed against his ear.

That look alone is enough to have my body locking tight in stone-cold fear. Something is definitely very wrong.

"Cage," I answer almost robotically.

"Greg! Oh, God. Greg…" She starts sobbing, and it takes every ounce of strength in my body to keep myself up and not crumpled into a mess on Sway's golden sidewalk.

"Dee," I gasp. There's a simple reason for her to be upset. I'm sure it's nothing.

"Hold…hold on. Let me…—let me put Beck on." Her words wobble and her breath hitches a few times before I hear Beck take the phone.

"Listen to me, brother."

I nod my head even though I know he can't see me. My whole body is about to shut down. I just look at Axel and beg him to make my fears unwarranted. His normally tan skin is pale, and his eyes are concerned and… full of agony.

NO! No, oh God… NO!

"Greg, I'm going to tell you something and I want you to keep your shit together, no matter how hard this is going to be. Axel's ready to help you. Let him."

"Just say it," I plead.

"There was an accident, Greg. Melissa and Cohen… Jesus, Cohen was taken by ambulance to the hospital. From what little I was able to get from one of the first responders on the scene, he's not badly injured."

I close my eyes. I know that my son is okay, but that relief is short-lived when I realize he's stopped talking and hasn't mentioned how my very pregnant wife is.

"John Beckett, you tell me right now that my wife, my fucking heart, is okay. Tell me right now that Melissa, Cohen, and my girls are okay!" I don't even attempt to wipe the tears that are falling down my face. Axel clamps his arm down on my shoulder, offering his support.

"She had to be airlifted out, Greg. You need to let Axel get you to the hospital as soon as you can. It…it doesn't look good."

I drop the phone, hearing it shatter against the sidewalk, and it isn't until I'm sitting in Axel's truck while he speeds down the interstate that I realize those terrifying wails I hear are coming from me.

CHAPTER 8

Melissa

TWO HOURS EARLIER

I HATE THAT Greg won't be with me for the shower. I know he said that he would try his best, but knowing *why* he got called in is making me crazier. Or I should say *who* is behind the reason he was called in. Everyone knows how that terrible Mrs. Hutchins is. She has her sights on all the men at Corps Security. I wouldn't even be shocked if she has tried to get some action from openly gay Davey. Greg's told me over and over how frustrating she is, and I know he'll be there longer than he wishes.

I don't pretend to understand why they keep her on as a client, but I trust my husband, so I'll give him the support he needs, even if I wish he were by my side right now.

I pull up to the intersection, adjusting my belt so that it doesn't keep digging into my belly, and take a deep breath. It doesn't do me any good to stress over a situation I can't control. I know it's my hormones making me insane. Seriously, I know that Greg doesn't have any interest in a baby shower. Hell, if I weren't the one with enough emotional crazy rushing through my veins right now, I would probably laugh at a husband being dragged to a shower for his pregnant wife. I know he doesn't care; he's just doing this because I want him there.

"Mommy, will I get presents too?"

I look away from the light a few cars ahead of me, still red, before looking up and focusing on Cohen's reflection in my rearview mirror.

I smile from just looking at his messy brown hair a few weeks past due for a cut, tousled just the way Greg's always is these days. His brown eyes, always bright with unshed energy, and that crooked smile never fail to melt my heart. I instantly want to start sobbing with the strength of my love for this little guy.

"Mommy, your face looks funny like it does when you cry. Are you going to cry? I don't have to get presents. I can wait till my birthday if you forgot them. Will Aunt Izzy have cake? I like leopards. Can we get my girls some leopards to match their sheets in their beds?" His smile gets bigger and he shakes his head rapidly.

"I love you, you know that?" I ask, smiling at him one more time before returning my eyes to the road when I see the light turn green.

"I know. I'm awesome."

"Yes, you sure are." I laugh, waiting for the car in front of me to go. I swear, traffic is a mess today. Apparently everyone and their mothers have somewhere they have to be.

"Can we buy a boat? I hope Aunt Izzy got a big cake. I'm going to eat it all up and get big like Maddox Locke."

"Cohen, you are so silly. Why don't you just call him Maddox?" Cohen's been calling Maddox by his full name for so long now that it's almost slipped out from my own lips a few times. Everyone thinks it's the cutest thing ever, but honestly, it's just another weird little piece of Cohen logic that helps make him the coolest kid around.

"Because."

"Because why?"

"Because Maddox Locke is cooler, and it makes me smile. Maddox Locke is funny. He told me that one day I'm going to be a big boy and I need to watch how Daddy acts so that I can be the bestest man in the whole world, just like Daddy. He says it's the key to being a superhero. Maddox Locke keeps his secrets all locked up. He told me that. But sometimes he unlocks his secrets and tells me some. So he's my Maddox Locke."

I have to take my eyes off the road and look at him. I've never noticed him and Maddox having conversations long enough for all that. Maddox is, for the most part, quiet and pensive. I've always known that he holds some deep pain, and while it's no secret with the girls that he's got a seriously secret soft side, this is the first I've heard of him and Cohen bonding like this.

"You know, he might be onto something there."

"I know."

I smile, focusing my attention back on the road when we finally start making some progress through the intersection that's been backed up for a while now.

"Uh, they need to do something about all this traffic," I mutter under my breath. They've been working on this intersection for what seems like years. The light that was a last-ditch effort to relieve some of the congestion seems to be making it worse. No one pays attention to anything.

Right when I'm about to cross over the intersection, I hear a loud horn followed by Cohen's scream in the backseat. Checking the car in front of me, seeing that it's a good distance ahead, I don't even get my eyes to the rearview to check the one following before I see it.

Just out of the corner of my eye, I see the flash of red before I hear the twisting, bending, moaning, and screaming sounds of metal and glass colliding. I can feel the tiny pieces of glass that fly from my window piercing my skin. My seatbelt pulls tight and digs into my skin. Every inch of my left side is on fire, burning in a way that makes my vision dim.

It takes only a second, but in that second, I think about the little boy in the backseat, praying that he's okay and unharmed. I pray that the little girls still growing in the safety of my belly aren't affected. And I think about the handsome man who isn't going to be okay if anything happens to his family.

"Co-hen…" I gasp when the car stops moving. My brain fights to understand where I am and why I can't open my eyes. Fighting every single fiber in my being that tells me to just let go and fade away.

I struggle to stay awake; I try to fight the pain and the fear. I beg my body to move, to stop just lying here and get to Cohen. He needs me, and I need to know he's okay.

I know it isn't going to be long now. I can feel my body slowly going numb, and the overwhelming pain starts to wash away when each part of my body becomes a stranger to me. My eyes keep rolling around in my head like they aren't attached anymore. My vision fades from color to black and gray, the webs of nothingness closing in and pulling me away.

"No… Co…hen…love."

Right before I feel the numbness crawl into my head, I hear the sweetest sound in the world.

I hear Cohen return my love. And even though he's crying, I know he's alive and that he knows that I love him.

CHAPTER 9

Greg

THE RIDE to the hospital is a complete and total wash. I don't see a single mile. I don't feel anything except soul-crushing pain. My family, my reason for living, is beyond my reach, and I wasn't there when they needed me.

My mind passed rational thinking about ten miles ago. Beck's words still echo like a badly scratched CD through my mind.

Accident.

It doesn't look good.

Airlifted.

I can feel the fear taking over. It doesn't matter how many times I beg and plead, pray and beg some more, I feel like I lost a piece of myself when he spoke those words.

Not knowing and fearing the worst but grasping on to that sliver of hope that keeps bursting through the darkness is the only thing keeping me from crumbling.

That and knowing that Cohen's going to need me...and I'm going to need him.

"We're almost there, brother."

Axel doesn't need me to respond. Hell, I'm not even sure if I could at this point.

The second I see the turn off for the hospital, I sit a little straighter in the seat. When I see the brick of the building pop through the trees, I lift my hand to the door handle. The second I feel his truck slowing, I unsnap my belt. And right when I see the doors to the emergency room, my door's released and I jump from the cab.

Luckily, Axel had already been slowing when I leaped from his moving truck, so there wasn't any resistance when I landed and took off at a dead sprint for the glass doors.

I can hear Axel screaming and cursing behind me, but I don't even pause. My body is driving me since my mind refuses to think. The only thought I'm capable of at this point is finding my boy and then my wife.

The little old lady sitting at the desk visibly shrinks back when I all but break down the wall to get into the hospital. Her eyes widen for a second before she catches herself and wipes her expression clear.

"Can I help—"

"Melissa and Cohen Cage. My family...please," I gasp, not even giving her the time to finish. I can feel the cool air on my wet cheeks, my tears once again flowing freely.

She looks down, glancing back up at me quickly before returning her eyes to her computer.

"Sir, I don't see—"

I sag with relief when Axel speaks from my side. "Melissa Cage, ma'am. Brought in by helicopter approximately fifteen minutes ago. Her son, also his son, Cohen Cage, should be arriving by ambulance either shortly after her or soon. Please, make the call and find out where he can find his family."

Even with his hand grasping my shoulder again, I can't feel it. That solid strength that he's trying to pass through to me is completely lost to my panic. I look around, praying that I'll see Melissa and Cohen in one of the many chairs around the room. Praying that this is some sick joke and my family is okay.

"Greg, let's go."

"Huh?" I look over at Axel's concerned expression, realizing that I missed the rest of his conversation.

"Let's go. Cohen's already here being seen and this nice nurse here, Lucy, is taking us to where he is." He points over to the nurse who's standing next to the desk, looking at me with the same expression of concern that Axel has on his face.

He doesn't have to tell me twice. The second I hear that I am about to hold my boy, I feel my heart start beating a little faster. Knowing that they wouldn't be taking me to him if he were badly injured is helping my fear recede some.

I watch the young nurse's ponytail sway with each rapid step she takes. I keep wanting to run past her and scream Cohen's name until I find him, but each time my pace gets too heavy, Axel clears his throat and grabs my arm. I feel like punching him in his goddamn arm for making me walk at this ridiculous pace. We should be running—hell, sprinting—through the halls.

"Right in here, Mr. Cage," Nurse Lucy states, opening the door to one of the emergency rooms.

I take a step toward the curtain that's pulled closed. I can hear movement, but I haven't heard my boy. I still feel the adrenalin pumping rapidly through my body, demanding that I rush, but now that I'm faced with not knowing what's on the other side of this blue barrier, I'm paralyzed in fear.

"Go. Now. I'll find someone who can give you some information on Melissa and go back out to the waiting room to see if anyone else is here yet." Axel gives me a shove before walking back down the hallway we just came down.

With a deep breath, I reach out and open the curtain. I couldn't have helped the sob that bubbles out audibly if I tried.

"Daddy!" His voice wobbles, and his chin quivers.

With one word, my body wakes up and I all but fall to his side. The nurse standing at his side jumps out of my way and allows me to fall to my knees next to the hospital bed that is all but swallowing his small body whole.

"Oh, God… Cohen."

"You can hold his right hand, sir. We're just about done with his left side."

I pull my eyes from Cohen's for the first time since opening the curtain and notice another person in the room working on stitching up part of his forearm. I can't see much more because of the angle, but I *can* see the amount of blood surrounding him, and it feels like a knife has just shot through my heart.

I don't even look up at the other nurse I almost ran over. I pick Cohen's hand up and press it to my lips, breathing in his scent.

"I couldn't help Mommy." His hand squeezes mine tight, his body shaking so hard that he's vibrating the bed.

"It's okay, baby. It's okay. Mommy's tough. She's going to be just fine."

Looking into his eyes, which are normally so full of life, and seeing the pain, fear, and stark, cold terror, I know he doesn't believe a word out of my mouth. If I'm honest with myself, I know that I sound more like I'm begging than I am reassuring.

"Miss? Is there any way I can get some information on his mother? My wife? She was in the accident as well." I look into Cohen's scared eyes, thankful that he's here and keeping me from tearing this hospital to the ground until I find Melissa.

"I'm sorry, but I don't have any information on the other person in the vehicle. Let me go see what I can find out."

It feels like an eternity while I sit there with Cohen, watching them stitch up different parts of his left arm. From what I can see, the worst of his injuries seem to be the millions of little cuts on almost every open surface of skin on his left side. He seems tired but otherwise just really banged up.

I take the first real breath I've breathed since I got Beck's call earlier.

Now I just need to know that Melissa and the girls are okay. It is literally killing me with each second that audibly ticks away from the clock in the corner. Without knowing, every single one of those seconds begins to feel like hope flying farther and farther away from my grasp.

It isn't long after they finished cleaning all his cuts and stitching up the deeper ones that Cohen fell asleep. I know it's the crash from the adrenalin and the pain medication that they gave him, but I hate it. I want to be able to see his eyes and know that he's okay.

I keep one hand around his and the other placed lightly on his stomach so that I can feel his breaths causing it to rise and fall.

And I wait.

I almost jump out of my skin when the door finally opens again and a forty-something doctor enters. His expression doesn't give anything away as he walks farther into the room, stopping at the foot of Cohen's bed. I stare into his dark blue eyes, both praying for the best and fearing the worst.

It isn't until I look down and notice 'OBGYN' on his white jacket that I feel something akin to terror crawl down my spine.

"Mr. Cage?"

I nod, afraid to speak.

"I'm Dr. Lowery. I know you're asking about your wife, and I apologize that I don't know more. About two hours ago, I performed an emergency Cesarean section on your wife. My job was to quickly deliver both of your daughters safely, and the last I heard, your wife is still in surgery. Both of your daughters are stable and in the NICU. Mr. Cage, I know you and your wife were told about the possibility that she wouldn't make it to term, but it's going to be a long road ahead for your daughters."

I close my eyes, feeling my despair fall one tear at a time down my face. I listen to every word that Dr. Lowery speaks. Steroids, feeding tubes, antibiotics, nasal CPAP, and monitors. I hear the words, but I don't understand them. My girls shouldn't be here yet, and no matter what he said earlier about Melissa being in surgery, the only thing that I can focus on is that if my girls had to be removed from their mother early, how badly is she injured?

"... see your daughters shortly."

"I'm sorry?" I have to force myself to look back up into his knowing eyes.

He smiles kindly and takes another step into the room. "I spoke with your son's doctor before coming in. He's lucky, and they'll be discharging him within the hour. We'll get you up to see your daughters shortly, Mr. Cage."

I just nod my head and watch him turn and leave. My mind is refusing to make sense of everything that's happening around me. The only thing keeping me from running through this whole damn building until I find Melissa and my daughters is the little banged-up boy sleeping in front of me.

With a deep breath and another silent prayer, I wait again.

With every minute that passes and still no word on Melissa, I feel more and more of my soul being stripped from my body. That hope I had earlier has become so small that I almost can't feel it anymore.

In the last hour, I've had nurses come in to check Cohen and Axel come back to update me on who is here and to tell me the same thing each time—no one will tell him anything. I've filled out a million and one pieces of paper, and now I just keep staring at the two bracelets the last nurse attached to my wrist.

I finger the bracelets, watching them spin around my wrist, and once again fight the urge to take off on a hunt for my family.

My daughters… My girls are here and fighting in some cold and sterile room. They're fighting to live and there isn't a damn thing I can do to protect them. Every instinct in my body is telling me to go into protector mode.

My wife, my beautiful and loving wife, is somewhere within these walls, and the unknown is tearing me apart.

"Daddy?" Cohen's soft whisper has me dropping my hands and looking over at him. "Will Mommy be okay?" His chin starts to tremble slightly.

"C-Man, can I tell you a secret?" He nods his head, a few tears slipping past his lids. "I'm going to teach you a trick. Remember when I told you that we always protect the women we love? Well, Mommy and your sisters need a special kind of protection. They need us to keep strong and share our strength with them. Every time you think about your mommy, you give her just a little more strength. And when you tell her you love her, it's even stronger. So right now, we're going to sit here and we're going to talk about every single thing we love about your mommy. And when we finish with that, we're going to talk about every single thing we can't wait to show your sisters. Then it won't be long before they have so much strength that they just can't help but get better."

And that's just what we do. I hold his little hand and we talk about every single thing we love about Melissa until they finally release Cohen from their care.

I hold it in, but deep down, I feel the bone-deep fear that I have no control over the outcome.

With my son in my arms, we walk out of the exam room and follow the nurse up to the NICU, where I'm told a doctor will find me shortly with news on the babies and Melissa.

My heart is somewhere in this hospital, and I can only hope and pray that everything will be okay.

CHAPTER 10

Greg

"**M**R. CAGE?" I jump when I hear my name being whispered. When I look around, it takes me a second to remember where I am, but when I do, it all comes crashing down at once.

Melissa.

The accident.

My girls, born and fighting for their lives.

Cohen, safe and scared.

Everything I thought set in stone for our happy lives together is hanging by a thread.

"I'm sorry, sir. I didn't mean to startle you." She smiles weakly, giving me a chance to get my bearings.

"It's okay. I didn't realize I had fallen asleep."

I look around, noting that Axel and Izzy are still in the same spot across the room. Dee's moved and is now lying with her head in Beck's lap. Asher is pacing, no doubt having a hard time being in the hospital so soon after losing his brother. Sway and Davey are seated in chairs, silently holding hands and waiting for the nurse to start talking.

Fortunately, Chelcie took Cohen home with her. It had been almost impossible for me to let him go, but I know he needs to be able to sleep and I need to be able to be here for Melissa.

"Would you like to come and see your daughters? I apologize for not being out here sooner. We've had a few other emergencies come in within the last hour that have kept me tied up."

For the first time since I got the call from Beck earlier, I feel a little bit of hope wash over my body.

"Yes…" I clear the emotions threatening to bubble over the top with a cough. "Yes, please. I need to see my girls."

She smiles and asks me to follow her. I take one more look around the room, meeting the eyes of my friends who have proven time and time again that we are just a big family. We love together, we fight together, and most importantly, we're there when one of us hits rock bottom with no hope of getting up again without support.

When we finally stop walking she asks me to put on a gown, a mask, and some stupid hat to cover my hair. I don't even question her. Knowing that my girls are just beyond the doorway has me rushing through all of her instructions.

The second I finish scrubbing what feels like every inch of my skin, I turn to her and wait. I try and calm my breathing, but knowing that I'm seconds away from meeting my daughters is making that next to impossible.

"Don't be alarmed by all the wires. They really are more intimidating than anything. Right now, they're doing remarkably well for being born this early. I was just looking at their charts before I came to find you. The doctor will go over it in more detail, but those two little girls are some strong little fighters."

I give her a weak smile, unable to express how much that means to me right now. Hearing that my girls have their mother's spirit helps that little seed of hope to grow a little larger.

Right before we step into the room I stop her, asking the one question I desperately need an answer to. "My wife, please... I need to know how she is."

"Let's get you in here to see your girls and I'll go chase down her doctor for you, okay?"

I nod, take a deep breath, and get ready to see my girls.

There is nothing in this world that can prepare you for the helplessness you feel at seeing your tiny babies with tubes and wires connected all over their small bodies. Everything about them terrifies me. But seeing them in their plastic incubator, the machines telling me that they are very much alive, gives me a small sliver of peace. I would give anything to be able to hold my girls, but for now I'll settle with the small hole I'm allowed to stick my hand through to feel their skin against my own.

I listen intently when the nurses explained everything they have attached to them and their care plan. Knowing that they have a long road ahead of them is made easier by knowing that there is a clear path to get to the finish line.

I spend the next thirty minutes in there looking at my princesses and stroking their tiny arms and hands, both just a little over three pounds of perfection, and giving my heart over to two more people.

I can't take my eyes off them, but when I hear a throat clear behind me, I finally allow myself to step away from my girls.

"Mr. Cage."

I look down at his lab coat. "Dr. Walsh." I turn to give my girls another look, bending forward and whispering softly to each of them through their incubator, "Be strong, my little warriors. Daddy loves you."

Once we step into the hall, Dr. Walsh turns to me and doesn't waste any time. "If you could follow me, I'll take you to your wife's room, Mr. Cage."

"She's...she's okay?"

He doesn't say anything for a long moment. He just looks at me with his expressionless eyes. "I'm going to be honest with you, Mr. Cage. Your wife is lucky to be alive. She's suffered extensive head trauma and has three broken ribs, a broken arm, and a broken leg. There was some internal bleeding that we were able to get under control rather quickly. Her head injury is the most important thing we're monitoring right now. We need to make sure we prevent the possibility of a secondary injury that could arise from here on. Your wife was unconscious when she arrived, and at the moment, we have her placed in a medically induced coma. We've discovered significant swelling of her brain as well as slight bleeding. So, like I said, that is our main concern right now. Our neurosurgery team will be monitoring the pressure in her brain with a bolt that was already placed and that will help guide the therapy as needed. We've started her on a medication called Keppra to prevent any seizures. I can only tell you that she's in good hands, Mr. Cage. We will be able to tell you more in the coming days, as the next twenty-four hours are the most critical."

My mouth opens, but no words came out. Trying to process all the medical vomit he just spewed all over me is taking too much energy. I grasp on to the only thing I can—knowing she's alive and that the rest will fall in place. I keep picturing her beautiful face telling me that she loved me earlier today. Or was it yesterday?

Silently, I nod my head and wait for the doctor to take me to my wife. With every step, I beg God to let me take her place.

CHAPTER 11

Greg

I THOUGHT I knew what it was like to live a nightmare.

When I lost Grace, I felt a pain that I hoped never returned.

When Cohen was kidnapped, I felt a hopelessness that crushed my soul.

When I saw my little girls, so achingly small, fighting for each breath, I felt a fear I'd never known I could possess.

When I walk into Melissa's hospital room and see her hooked to machines, bruised and battered… I feel a little piece of myself die.

I'm living a nightmare that I can only pray I wake up from.

It's hard to put into words how you feel when you see the love of your life like that. I watch her chest rise with each breath, giving me the reassurance that she's still with me, but looking at her so obviously broken has my knees buckling before I had make it more than five feet into the door.

I feel the doctor pause, waiting to see if he needs to assist me, but I wave him off. Dropping my hands to the floor and letting my head hang, I pray. I scream and plead, once again, for God's mercy. I can't lose Melissa. There's no other alternative for me. She's mine, and I won't let anyone take her.

I pull in a deep breath, holding it while I get my courage back together before picking myself off the floor and walking over to the side of her bed.

And that's where I stay, holding her hand and caressing her soft skin while I listen to the doctor go on and on about her injuries. I try to understand what he is telling me, but with each word that passes his lips, I realize just how very real this is.

His heavy hand settles on my shoulder, but I can't look away from her beautiful face, I'm trying to see past the swelling and bruises to glimpse the woman I kissed goodbye hours before.

"… time will tell, Mr. Cage. For now, we will monitor your wife closely for changes."

I look up when I hear him leaving, the door closing softly behind him, and I sit there in the dim light of Melissa's hospital room and start singing. At first, it's anything I can think of that she might like, but after a few songs, I just start the humming familiar melody Adele's 'Make You Feel My Love' over and over. The words start to flow without thought while my thumb rubs in small circles against her wrist, my tears rolling down my face unchecked.

God, what the hell do I do now?

CHAPTER 12

Cohen

I DON'T LIKE this place. It smells funny, and everyone looks sad. I just want my mommy and daddy. Aunt Izzy told me this morning that it's okay to be scared and that she was there if I needed a hug. I don't need a hug. I'm a big boy.

I've been sitting here for a really long time, long enough to watch three shows on Uncle Axel's phone. I hope Daddy comes to get me soon.

The doctors and nurses always run around here like they forgot to turn the oven off. Mommy always does that a lot. Uncle Axel and Aunt Izzy are here watching me, but Nate stayed home with Dilbert and Davey. Aunt Izzy said that Nate is too little to be here. Uncle Beck and Aunt Dee went to go get me some breakfast, but I didn't want to go with them because I'm waiting on my daddy to come and get me. I'm going to see my mommy soon.

I heard Aunt Izzy on the phone this morning when Daddy called. She didn't think I could hear her, but she was being loud like Aunt Dee gets when she talks about her silly shoes. She told Daddy that I'm being such a good little boy and that she would take me to him if he really wanted her to. It's been almost two weeks since my mommy went to sleep and Daddy started sleeping at the hospital with her. I don't know how long that is, but that's what Aunt Izzy said. It feels like a really long time.

I miss them, but I don't tell anyone because I'm being strong like Daddy.

I don't know why I wouldn't want to go to my daddy. He makes everything okay. I want to yell at Aunt Izzy when she calls me a little boy. I'm not a little boy. I'm a big boy, and I'm going to use all of my powers to make everything better.

Last night I came to see Daddy and I really didn't want to leave. My side still hurts, and I'm itchy where they had to tie my skin with little strings after Mommy's car broke. Mommy would have made it not hurt anymore. Aunt Izzy doesn't kiss my boo-boos like Mommy does.

Now I'm sitting here in the stinky hospital, waiting on my daddy to come and take me to see my girls. No one will tell me where my sisters are. Aunt Izzy says that they have to sleep in a special clear box like Snow White did so that the germs don't hurt them while they get healthy. I don't like my girls sleeping in a box. They need to get better so I can teach them everything I know.

I'm going to teach them how to fight the bad guys, find the best rocks, where Mommy keeps her chocolate, how to paint and color, all the things that make Mommy and Daddy smile, and all the things that make Mommy and Daddy really laugh. Yup, they need to get better so I can teach them everything I know!

I kick my legs some more, letting them swing really fast, and think about how I can make my girls' box better.

"Hey, C-Man." I jump when I hear the deep voice, but I smile when I see who it is.

"You scared me, Maddox Locke." Daddy said that he's been chasing Aunt Emmy and he's going to bring her back to us, so I don't know why he's here. I don't like the way he keeps looking at me either. Everyone keeps looking at me like they don't know what to do with me.

"Brought you something, Cohen."

I look up and see some red stuff in Maddox Locke's hand. I can't wait to get a present. This place doesn't have anything fun to do. When he unfolds it, I see a cape just like the one the ambulance man cut off of me the other day. I want to smile.

I haven't smiled since Mommy fell asleep when that truck hit her car. I don't want to smile. But now I can. I have my power back, and I can help my mommy and my girls.

"Thank you, Maddox Locke."

"You're welcome, Cohen Cage."

He sits down next to me and helps tie my cape around my neck. It feels good to have my magic back. When I didn't have my cape and my mommy wasn't there, I got really scared. I didn't tell Daddy, but I didn't like being scared.

"You know what's going on?"

I shake my head at him. "I know Daddy is at the hospital because Mommy is sleeping and my sisters are out of her belly."

"That's right, C, and right now your daddy needs to be there for them because they need him real bad. I know you're really strong so they're going to need you too, but little dudes can't sleep at hospitals so I'm going to stay with you for a little while. If that's okay?"

"Do I still get to see Daddy and our girls?"

Maddox Locke smiles and I smile back, but I don't know why we're smiling.

"Yeah, buddy. Your daddy will be out here after he finishes talking to the morning doctor and then we can see about seeing *your* girls."

"Okay! Thank you, Maddox Locke. I'm happy you're home."

I feel better now. I pull the sides of my cape over my shoulders and close my eyes when I feel it tighten across my back. Taking a deep breath, I open my eyes and wait for Daddy so we can take care of our girls.

We don't get to see my girls right away. Daddy comes out and hugs me for a really long time. I see him every day, and every day he hugs me like this. Sometimes he squeezes me so hard it hurts just a little, but I like it. Daddy's hugs always make my sad stop.

"Daddy, do I get to see my girls today?"

He smiles big, but he still looks sleepy. If Mommy wasn't sleeping she would make him take a nap so he didn't turn into a grump.

"Yeah, C-Man. I bet we can make that happen today. I'm going to go up and see them in a little while, so I'll ask the doctor if we can work something out. Do you think it would be okay for Maddox to sit with you while you visit with Mommy today? Just while I run up to see your sisters?"

"Okay, Daddy. I'll take good care of Mommy while you go see

Lila and Lyn." I really want to see my sisters, but I want to spend some time with Mommy.

"Lila and Lyn, huh?" He smiles and for the first time in a lot of days, his smile doesn't look sad.

"Yup!"

He hugs me again and then picks me up to take me to see my mommy.

Maddox Locke got really bored while I talked to Mommy, so I let him play Flappy Birds on my iPod. I laughed really hard when he got so mad that he threw my iPod. Especially when he called Aunt Dee and asked her to stop at the store to buy me a new one.

"Sorry I broke your toy, Cohen, but Dee's going to bring you a new one in just a little while… Hey, why don't we keep this between us?"

"Maddox Locke, you're lucky my mommy didn't see you throw a fit or you would be in time out for a reallllly long time." I laugh when his face turns red like Mommy's does when Daddy says stuff in her ear.

"Right. Wouldn't want to be in time out, little dude. I'm going to step into the bathroom, remember not to touch any of the cords, okay?"

I wait until he steps into the bathroom before I look back at Mommy. She looks so pretty when she sleeps, even if she still has some bumps and cuts. She's still the most beautiful mommy in the whole world.

"I love you, Mommy. You're going to wake up and be so proud of Daddy and me. I've been eating all my vegetables and cleaning up my messes. I stay with Aunt Chelcie some. Just when Aunt Izzy has to work and stuff. I don't know why because Aunt

Izzy just plays on her computer. Aunt Chelcie doesn't really know what to do with me all the time. She cries a lot too, but says it's horn moans. I haven't heard of those before, but I hope I never get them. I wish you would wake up, Mommy."

She doesn't wake up.

I keep wishing she would though.

"I'm going to see my sisters soon. Daddy said they are really small, but I'm still going to love them."

I take a deep breath, scoot really close to Mommy without touching her cords, and start whispering the words I know will make her happy.

"What are you singing, Cohen?"

I heard Maddox Locke come back in from the bathroom when I was in the middle of my song, but I couldn't stop. Mommy needs to hear all the words to get better.

"Singing Daddy's song. He sings it to her every single day. He told me that Mommy can hear him singing and she will know how much he loves her, so I'm singing Mommy his song so she knows how much I love her. Did you know that our love is going to make her all better?" I smile big at Maddox Locke, because I know I'm right. Soon she's going to wake up and it's going to be because of our love.

"You know, I think you're onto something, little dude. Why don't you teach me the words so I can help you out?"

I don't know how long we sit here, but Maddox Locke helps me sing Daddy's song to Mommy so many times I get so tired I fall asleep.

CHAPTER 13

Greg

I HAVE TO stop at the door of Melissa's room before entering when I hear Cohen's words to Maddox. It never fails to amaze me just how perfect my son is. I can't imagine how he is feeling through all of this. Not only with Melissa's situation, but with having to stay with Izzy and Axel, sometimes with Chelcie, for the last two weeks. He hasn't complained, not one damn word, but deep down I know he's scared. Hell, *I'm* scared out of my fucking mind. If I could keep him here with me every second I would, but between Melissa and the girls, I'm stretched thin. There are two floors between us, but it feels like an ocean.

This morning I got the best news I have received since this nightmare began. The swelling on Melissa's brain is completely gone. The doctors keep telling me that we're in the home stretch. All her scans look great, her vitals are getting stronger and stronger daily, and her other injuries are healing well. Now we're just waiting for her to wake up.

I miss her more than I ever thought was possible. I've only left her side to go see the girls. It's like having my chest split open each and every time I have to leave Melissa to go to the girls, and it's just as bad when I leave the girls to come back to Melissa. She wouldn't want them up there alone, and as much as I want to stand by her bedside and guard her sleeping body, I know where I'm needed the most right now.

My girls need me, but I know they need their mother more.

Lillian is such a champ; she definitely takes after Melissa with her fighter's spirit. She's been the one I know, in my gut, I don't have to be concerned about. Even in this short time, I can see little differences in her. She doesn't look as tiny and breakable as she first did. Don't get me wrong though. She's still so little I'm afraid to breathe around her, but she's a born fighter.

Lyndsie, on the other hand, worries me. I can feel her pain, her struggles, and I crave the ability to take them from her, to heal her. Like her sister, her lungs aren't developed. A few days after she was born, she had to be placed on a CPAP machine because one of her little lungs collapsed. I didn't sleep one wink that night. She's been able to come off of it now, but that still doesn't stop my fears of something else going wrong. Luckily, she seems to be turning a corner. Our most recent struggle is her reflux and her inability to gain weight. This morning I had more good news from the doctors when they said that Lyndsie hadn't had any episodes, and kept all her feedings down.

Thank Christ.

I do what I can. I stay strong when all I want to do is break down. I visit all three of my girls. I hold Melissa's hand while I sing and talk to her. I reach through the girls' incubators and run my finger across their silky skin, avoiding all the wires, singing softly to them and telling them how much we love them.

"Hey."

I look up from where I was staring at my feet, and meet Maddox's hard but sad eyes. He's never been one to show his emotions, but he would have to be completely heartless to be unaffected by this whole situation.

"Hey," I breathe.

"How are you feeling? And don't give me any shit, Greg. There isn't any way in hell that you're this calm on the inside." He props up against the wall next to Melissa's door and just waits.

I could ignore him like I've ignored everyone else but Cohen.

"I'm falling apart, brother. I've had to keep my shit locked so tight I feel like someone locked me in a cage and threw away the key. Part of me wants to let loose, uncage the beast I can feel pacing inside me. I want to run through the halls, demanding answers and quick fixes. Goddamn, I just want my girls better and all of this to just be one big nightmare."

He doesn't say much for the longest time. He just presses his lips into a thin line. If it weren't for the rapid drumming of the veins in his neck, I would think he's the picture of calm and collected. But I know better. I know how much it costs him to just be inside a hospital.

"You remember how it was after I got hurt? You can't rush these things, Greg. And as much as I wish you could… Well, she'll wake up when her body is ready. Doctors are telling you her brain is ready, scans are showing she's ready, but mentally she's locking herself up tight until *she* is ready. I don't talk about what it was like for me all those months in the hospital after the attack. You know because you were on my team, but the only reason I pulled through was because I thought I had a reason to wake up. Keep talking to her and remind her *why* she needs to come back."

I haven't heard Maddox speak about the bombing that essentially ended his military career for years. Hell, it's probably been close to ten now, but damn if it doesn't give me a spark of hope.

"You know, I don't know how you always know the right shit to say, but thank you. I've been struggling, Mad. Struggling so hard I don't even know how to get past this bump in the road. I feel like I'm letting everyone down. Even Cohen. God, Maddox…he's been so brave, and I can't even offer him any kind of promise that his mother and sisters will be okay. How the hell am I going to get past this shit?"

"That's the easy part. Hike your goddamn big boy panties up and you be the hero that little boy knows you are."

"Daddy?"

I jump slightly when I hear Cohen's voice, my brows creasing in concern when I hear his tone, but the second I see his eyes shining with hope, I push myself off the wall and drop down onto my knees in front of him.

"Hey, C-Man. Are you okay?"

"Daddy," he whispered so softly that I almost didn't hear him.

"Cohen?" I question, starting to panic slightly.

"Daddy!" Tears begin to pile in his lids, causing my heart to beat at a pace so rapid I fear it might pop right out of my chest.

I feel Maddox move past me into Melissa's room but keep my eyes focused on Cohen.

"It happened," His body starts shaking with his gasping breath, and I wrap my arms around him, pulling him into my arms.

"Cohen, please talk to me. I don't—" I don't get to finish my thought because I am interrupted when Maddox rushes back into the hallway. One look at his face and I know something has happened.

I scoop Cohen up in my arms and rush past a stunned Maddox, my feet almost too heavy to pick up, but when I get to into the room, I stop dead in my tracks.

My chest burns; it burns so badly. I don't even attempt to stop the tears that are rapidly falling down my face. I don't even notice Cohen squirming to get down until Maddox pulls him out of my hold. It isn't until I feel his weight leave my body that I drop to the floor with a howl of relief so loud I swear the windows shake.

I quickly pick myself off the floor and keep my eyes locked on the hospital bed my wife is lying on still. When I see Melissa's beautiful blue eyes staring sleepily back at me, I rush to her side, pressing kisses all over her forehead and sobbing like a baby.

The next thirty minutes are a rush of activity. Doctors and nurses run in and out of the room. Her vitals are checked and re-checked. They move cords, unhook machines, and give her more medication. The whole time, her eyes never leave mine. I can see the worry, fear, and confusion all rolling around behind her eyes. I want to hurry to her side, but I keep my feet rooted to the floor where the doctor demanded I stand.

I nod my head when they explain to me what is going on, I grunted when answers are demanded, and the whole time I keep her gaze. I never leave her line of sight; it is just the two of us in a room full of chaos.

"Greg," she whispers, her voice low, gravely, and unused.

I can tell it caused her pain to even talk, so I move quickly to her side, grabbing her hand and dropping my head against the bed next to her hip.

"I'm here, Beauty. God, I'm here. I love you. I love you so damn much. Thank you for coming back to us." My body is shaking with the force of my emotion. I can feel her fingertips lightly moving against my cheek. Even though her body is drained of energy, she's still trying to fight through the darkness to comfort me.

There is no way in hell I deserve this woman.

"Babies," she rasps again. "My… bab—"

"Shh, now. The girls… God, the girls are perfect. Just like I knew they would be. They look just like you, Beauty. Just like you. Perfectly perfect."

Tears leak from the corners of her eyes, sliding silently down her face. She smiles weakly before she closes her eyes and her breathing deepens.

I frantically look around before my eyes settle on a young nurse standing at the foot of her bed. Her eyes are wet, and she's holding her hand against her chest like she's in pain.

"Please! Help her! She can't… Why isn't she awake?! Help, please!" My panic is starting to consume me, and the little burst of joy that just flooded my system is dying.

"Daddy, Mommy is just taking a nap now. Doctor said so. He said Mommy would be tired and her body needed more sleep. That's silly though because Mommy's been asleep for a million days!"

"She's okay, brother. It's time to release that breath you've been holding for *a million days*."

I laugh when Maddox stops talking. I laugh for the first time in weeks. It sounds rusty, and I'm sure I look like a complete fool.

But I laugh. I keep laughing as Cohen climbs into my lap and laughs with me.

And then I take that breath that I've been holding since this all started.

I take that breath, pull my son close, and let the floodgates fly open. Every ounce of fear I've had consuming my body comes rushing to the surface so that the joy I'm feeling has room to take its place.

CHAPTER 14

Cohen

MOMMY IS awake now.

I've been really scared, but I've been a big boy and didn't tell anyone. I didn't want anyone to know.

But I used my magic and sang Mommy her song and it worked. It worked!

Now it's time to use my magic on my girls.

I just know it's going to work too, because my girls know. They *know* that I'm their big brother and I'll never ever *ever* let anything hurt them.

"Daddy. I need to see my girls now. It's time."

Daddy looks at me with a really funny face. I've never seen him do that face before, but it's really funny. It's the face that Uncle Axel always makes when Dilbert is running around in those really tall shoes that Aunt Dee wears. They look like they hurt really bad, but Dilbert is always running around like a funny man. Uncle Axel makes that face, kinda like he swallowed a fly and he doesn't know how to get it out.

"Daddy. We need to go now."

He looks at Mommy again and then up at Maddox Locke before he looks back at me. "Right now, C-Man?"

"Yes, Daddy. Right this minute."

"All right then. Let's go see if we can get them to open the curtain for you."

I don't like the sounds of that. I don't want to look into the curtain anymore. I want to touch my sisters so they can feel my magic, but I guess I can figure out another way.

I jump down from Daddy's lap and hold my hand out for him. He shakes his head, and I smile when he holds my hand, stands, and gets ready to leave.

"You'll find me if she wakes up before we get back?" he asks Maddox Locke.

"Yeah."

I turn back and look at Maddox Locke; he smiles big and winks at me. I smile back, really big, because Maddox Locke doesn't smile a lot, but when he does, it's really cool.

"Cohen, what are we doing?"

I finish untying my cape from around my neck. It's not the same as my old one, but I know it has my magic on it because I haven't taken it off once since Maddox Locke tied it around my shoulders.

"I'm going to fix my sisters."

I know Daddy doesn't understand, but I just smile and hand

him my cape.

"Uh, okay?" He looks down at me. His face is funny again. And then he looks at my cape in his really big hand. "What do you want me to do with this, buddy?"

"My girls need it. But you have to tell them that it's from their big brother. They *have* to know that it's from me or the magic won't work."

"Cohen, son… I need you to clear it up for me because I'm a little confused."

"Daddy, you have to stay with me here." He laughs, but I keep going. This is important. "You need to take my magic in there. My girls are in their box and they need my magic!"

Why doesn't he understand? If I could go in there and do it myself, I would, but they won't let me in there. They say I have to stay out here because I might have germs.

"All right, Cohen… Let me see what I can do." He waves over the nice nurse lady who always smiles at me. I can't hear what they say when she steps out of the room my girls are in, but I really don't like her funny face.

I want to yell when Daddy hands her my cape, but I keep quiet and watch her walk back into the room. I can see my girls sleeping in the same box. I hate them in that glass box.

He picks me up and holds me high so that I can see in the room a little better. I keep watching as the nurse weaves through the stuff in her way until she reaches my girls.

The nurse looks over and smiles at us again. I hold my breath when she takes my cape and lays it across my girls' glass box. She smiles again, waves, and gives me a thumbs up.

I look over at Daddy. His face looks funny again, but this time his eyes are wet. That's okay; I won't tell anyone that he cried. I smile again because this time I know that everything is going to be just perfect.

CHAPTER 15

Melissa

S OFT SINGING pulls me from my dreams—that beautiful, deep baritone I've heard in my dreams for what seems like ages. The feeling of love drips from each word, instantly warming my soul and easing my mind.

It takes me a few minutes to understand where I am and why I hear my husband singing to me about going to the ends of the earth, and it makes me feel his love. Why my eyelids feel as if they weigh a hundred pound each, my body is sluggish to my commands, and almost every inch of my body hums with pain.

I briefly remember opening my eyes earlier and seeing Greg in a hospital room. It's hazy, but I remember him, Cohen, and Maddox standing right inside the doorway…and then nothing else.

In those minutes, I noticed one thing with stark clarity. I didn't feel my babies. The pressure and dull pain I had become accustom to over the course of my pregnancy, the rolling of their bodies, the jabs and kicks—all of it was gone. I can feel my panic starting to peak, knowing that there is something gravely wrong if my babies aren't here.

Oh, God!

In little flashes, like a projector playing slides of my last moments of consciousness, I remember.

Cohen being Cohen, making me laugh with his innocence and wonky train of thought. Looking up in the mirror to meet his smiling eyes. Driving through the green light and that terrible sound of horns and colliding metal. Screams from my boy and his sobbing voice telling me he loves me.

Then it all fades to black.

Cohen! My sweet boy! Where is my sweet boy?

Oh, God... My girls. It's too early for them to be out. They still need time!

My ribs burn when my panic starts to escalate. I hear beeping speed up, and those words that were singing earlier stop abruptly.

Then I feel him.

His hands hold my head between them, his warm breath fanning across my face when he speaks, calming me instantly.

"Beauty, my sweet Beauty, calm yourself. Everything is going to be fine. Everything *and* everyone... You're all safe, my love." His lips press against mine for a second before he's gone.

I try to open my eyes, but they burn. I try to speak, but my throat feels like I've been eating dirt and glass. I try to move my arm, but it drops worthlessly.

"Shh. Let the nurse look at you, and I'll be right here," I hear Greg say from far away, his voice reassuring but thick with emotion.

I slow my breathing and try to calm down my body. He said

that everyone is fine. He wouldn't have said that if something had happened to our children.

But where are they?

Movement continues around me. My body is poked and moved around. I painfully answer all of her questions and try to remain calm until I feel my husband's hands on my skin again.

I need him.

I need his touch.

And I need his love.

It feels like an eternity, but it's probably only ten minutes before I am given some small sips of water and moved to a more comfortable position. My vision is still blurry, but I can see him. The second I see his face, that perfectly handsome face I love so much, I feel a sob bubble out. It hurts—oh it hurts more than I could have fathomed. Not just my screaming ribs, but low on my abdomen, the muscles feel unused and pulled tight.

I see his smile, and even with the tears running silently down his face, that smile never dims. I can tell that he hasn't slept—his eyes look tired, rimmed red, and swollen. His clothing is wrinkled and stained. He looks...terrible, and it's the most incredible sight I've ever seen.

"You look like crap," I rasp, smiling up at him as he walks over to the side of my bed.

He laughs, although it comes out more like a sob. "You don't say?"

"Doesn't your wife iron your clothes?" I joke weakly.

His tears stop, and the fear leaves his eyes.

"No, she likes me better naked."

The nurse I wasn't aware was still in the room snickers from where she's standing while she enters data into the computer connected to the wall.

"Lucky woman, that wife of yours," I whisper, my voice still gravelly in a painful way, but I feel my smile grow when he dips and moves his face closer to mine.

"I think I'm lucky one, my beautiful wife." His lips close the distance again, pressing against mine and peppering loving kisses against my lips and face.

He doesn't make a move to deepen the kiss. He just keeps raining his love across my face.

When he pulls away, he wipes my tears away with his thumbs. I try to move my hand again, but I break eye contact when I feel the solid weight surrounding it. I see the cast just seconds before I notice my very obvious empty belly.

And I'm right back to where I was minutes before.

"Oh, God! Greg… Cohen and the babies!" My panic rises again.

"Hey… Melissa, calm down. Please. You don't need to be working yourself up so soon. They're okay. I promise you. Cohen is with Axel and Izzy. He'll be back as soon as visiting hours start in the morning. It got too late for him to stay, so they took him home to get some sleep. The girls, both of them… They're okay and close by in the NICU."

It takes a few seconds for his words to bleed into my panic-fog, but when they do, I fall back against the mattress and pillow and sob.

The tears fall rapidly. I gasp for breath, causing sharp pains to shoot from my ribs and abdomen. And through it all, Greg continues to whisper his love and reassurance.

My children are alive.

Everything is going to be okay.

I've got my husband with his arms around me, pouring every ounce of strength he possesses into my body while he kisses my forehead and whispers softly in my ear. My son isn't hurt and being cared for by people we trust. And my daughters are here, safe and *alive*!

"I need to see them, Greg. I need to see our babies!" I have no idea if he can understand me, but he nods and promises me that as soon as the doctors allow it he will take me to our girls.

"You wouldn't believe it, Beauty, but they look just like you. So tiny, but absolutely the most precious and beautiful babies in the world." He pulls out his phone and holds it so that I can see picture after picture of our daughters. When he gets to one of him holding one of their tiny bodies against his naked chest, his whole hand almost swallowing her small body, I lose it again.

"Hey, they're okay. This is Lyndsie. She's had the harder time between the two of them, but every time I'm able to hold her skin to skin, she eats better. She hasn't been able to suck well, and she has some reflux problems, but she's doing great, Beauty. I held her earlier for a while just like this. Lillian, oh baby—she is a warrior. The doctors think she'll go home before Lyndsie because she's breathing on her own now and eating well. She's gaining weight quickly. I bet she's a chunk before we know it."

I suck up each word he speaks while he flips through hundreds of pictures of our little girls. I can hear the pride in his voice when he speaks about them. I push back the jealousy I feel when he talks about holding them. I need to see my babies, to feel my babies, so I know that they're okay.

"… so good, Beauty. You did so good." He drops the hand holding his phone, and I look over to him, smiling when I see the happiness in his eyes. "I was so scared, Melissa. So scared that I would never get this. Every day you slept, I worried more and more. The doctors kept telling us that you would wake up when you were ready, but God…I was so scared."

"How long was I out?" It feels like I just went to sleep hours ago, but the way he speaks, it's been a lot longer.

"Two weeks. Two long weeks."

"Oh my God."

"You're here now, and we just need to focus on getting all my girls out of this damn place and home. I need my family home."

We spend the rest of the night and into the morning whispering softly to each other in between small bouts of my sleeping. Every time I wake up, he's still sitting in the same chair, his crystal blue eyes just watching me sleep.

Finally, sometime when the sun is creeping into the sky, I open my eyes from another nap to see his head against my thigh and hear soft snores echoing through the room.

CHAPTER 16

Melissa

"**I**'M SO nervous." I look over at Greg, who is standing against the wall of the elevator as it climbs the two floors that will take me to my girls. "So damn nervous," I whisper again.

"Stop, Melissa. Once you see those two little princesses, all of those nerves will just wash away. When you feel their soft skin against your own, look at their small faces that are little mini versions of your own…all of that will just vanish, and the love you'll feel take its place is like nothing you have ever felt."

I have to blink away the tears that his words cause. My nose burns with the force of my emotions.

The doors open and Greg takes his place behind my chair, pushing me onto the floor where my girls are. With every step he takes, my wheelchair moving closer and closer, I feel like I can sense my girls. Like my body knows that I'm nearing my daughters.

We stop so that he can help me wash what feels like my whole body and push my arms through the gown I have to wear. It's hard with my cast to get everything situated, and by the time we finish, my frustration is strong. I just want to see my babies. I'm so close to my girls.

"I can see your mind working. We'll be in there in just a minute, but we have to follow the steps to make sure they are safe, Beauty."

I know he's right, but that doesn't stop the irrational mama bear that just wants her little cubs in her arms.

We finally get situated and he helps wheel me into the room. I know which incubator holds my girls before we're even all the way into the room. I see Cohen's bright red cape with its royal blue trim like a flag waving me home draped across one of the incubators.

"He wanted his *magic* in here. You should have seen him, Melissa. He had so much determination to get that in here so that he could save his sisters with his powers. That boy is something else. He's been amazing the last two weeks. So strong."

"That sounds just like him." I smile but never move my eyes from the flash of red in the otherwise very dull room.

He pushes me closer until I'm eye level with the two little babies nestled close to each other inside the small incubator. I don't even realize I am crying until I feel Greg wiping the tears from my face.

"They're beautiful," I whisper in awe.

"They sure are."

I just keep looking at them, taking in every single feature on their bodies as I feel the instantaneous love take over my nerves—just like Greg said it would.

"I need to feel them, Greg. I need to hold my babies."

He nods his head before he walks over to the nurse who is standing not that far from us and speaks softly. I can't hear what he's saying to her and I honestly don't care as long as it gets my babies in my arms.

We spend a while trying to figure out how to maneuver things so that I am able to hold my daughters. With my cast, it isn't possible to hold them both at the same time, so Greg helps the nurse place Lillian in my arms. The first time I feel her against my skin, I weep. I try to keep it together, but when that featherweight is pressed against my chest... I lose it. Greg stays close, keeping one hand against Lillian's back and the other arm draped across my shoulders.

I hold her for about ten minutes before Greg takes over and the nurse helps move Lyndsie into my arms. Just like with Lillian, I bawl. Completely lose it. Greg pulls one of the rockers next to my wheelchair and sits next to me while he cradles Lillian against his strong chest.

"They're so small, Greg. You swear they're going to be okay?"

"I promise, Beauty."

I smile.

He smiles back, leans in, and kisses me lightly.

I place a kiss on Lyndsie's downy head, locking eyes with Greg as he does the same to Lillian.

We sit there a little while longer until the nurse comes up and asks if we would like her to take a picture for us.

And with my girls safe in our arms, my husband by my side, and a love big enough to smother you, we take the first picture with our daughters.

"I can't wait to get one of those with Cohen."

"You and me both."

"Soon?"

Greg looks over at my question, that big smile from last night back on his face. "Soon," he vows.

EPILOGUE

Greg

THREE MONTHS LATER (CHRISTMAS)

"**D**ADDY! DADDY! DADDY!" Cohen's warm breath hits my ear and his whisper is loud enough to wake the dead.

I groan, knowing that there is no way Cohen's going to sleep anytime soon. I feel like I just fell asleep seconds ago, which isn't far from the truth.

"C-Man, what are you doing awake?"

"Got things to do, Daddy!" Jesus, he's starting to sound more and more like Maddox daily. Ever since they bonded when the girls were in the hospital, I feel like my son is turning into a Locke clone.

"Son."

"Daddy."

Melissa snickers next to me, and I know she gets a kick out of our four-year-old turning into some little mini alpha boy.

"Cohen, why don't we go to sleep for just a few more minutes?" *Or hours*, I silently add.

"Can't."

"Annnnd why can't we do that?" I finally peek my eyes open and jump when I realize how close he is to my face. "Jesus, son, do you have to sneak up like that?"

He giggles softly. "I didn't sneak up on you. I was just talking to you, Daddy. We have to go… Go now!"

"Okay, okay." I throw back the covers, remembering a second too late that I'm still naked from taking Melissa just a few hours before.

"HA! Daddy has his wiener rings in! Daddy, your wiener is funny looking with Mommy's earrings in there!" He starts dancing around the room, chanting about my goddamn wiener rings.

Melissa sits up and starts laughing uncontrollably. I look over at her and notice that the sheet has pooled around her waist about the same time Cohen does. I hold my breath…waiting for it.

"Mommy! Boobies! Mommy has boobies. Boobies. Boobies! Ha ha ha! I want Lucky Charms for breakfast! Let's go! I'll go get my girls!"

It's my turn to laugh now. Melissa is blushing about ten shades of red, and I'm standing in the middle of the bedroom, naked as the day I was born, laughing at my wife.

As hectic as my life is between Cohen and all his crazy fun, two little girls who seem to do nothing but wake and eat with a little sleep sprinkled in there, and a full-time job, it's moments like this that make me realize just how lucky we are and just how blessed we are to be here.

It hasn't been easy. Melissa had to stay in the hospital for two weeks after she woke up. The doctors wanted to make sure that she was completely cleared before they would release her, and I was okay with that.

Lillian was able to come home with Melissa, exactly a month after she was born. She's such a strong little girl. Taking Melissa and Lillian home was bittersweet. In one hand, it felt so good to have them home, but I think we all felt the hole from that not having Lyndsie home with us left.

It was for almost three weeks full of daily hospital visits later that we were able to take Lyndsie home. She had issues with her reflux that just kept setting us back, but finally, almost two months after she was born, we were able to bring her home and complete the Cage family.

Cohen took to his sisters instantly. He helps with everything he can. He holds the bottles while we feed them; he talks to them and sings to them. And every night he tells them everything he's going to teach them when they get older.

I love watching them interact. Knowing that he feels the need to protect his sisters makes me smile. Those poor girls are going to love when they get older and have two shadows over them. There's no way in hell that Cohen or I will let anything happen to our two princesses.

Melissa finally got her casts off both her arm and leg removed about a month ago. She's had some issues with gaining her full strength back, but she keeps at her physical therapy, determined to heal.

It hasn't been the easiest of times, but we're together, and I'll take a bumpy road over the alternative any day.

Melissa and I get ready in a comfortable silence, listening to Cohen chatter in the girls' room through their baby monitors.

"Come on, my Beast. Let's go get that crazy boy out of the nursery before he wakes up the girls. Good thing they can sleep through anything."

She starts walking out of the room, only limping slightly, and my mouth waters when I see the yoga pants she's put on hugging her perfect ass.

Ever since we got the go-ahead from the doctors, we've been almost insatiable. Doesn't take a doctor to tell me that I'm channeling my fear from almost losing her into sex. Melissa isn't complaining. If my diving into her sweet body daily gives my mind peace, she's more than happy to help out there.

I have to give myself a few minutes to calm down before I can follow her out of the room. Just one glance at her tight body and I'm ready to lock the door and throw her back on the bed.

"Come on, Cohen. Let the girls sleep some more." I smile when her voice comes over the monitor, before I finally walk out of our bedroom and down into the kitchen to start breakfast.

They follow not long after I started cooking, and even though Cohen starts to fuss over Lucky Charms, he eats the eggs, bacon, and pancakes quickly before asking for seconds.

"Daddy! Did you see? I looked out my window this morning and there's a gigantic trampoween out there! Santa brought it. I knew he would! Can I have a motorcycle when I get older? Maddox Locke has one!"

Jesus, it's hard to follow his train of thought sometimes.

"Why don't we talk about that when you're old enough?"

"Okay. Can I get wiener rings yet?"

Melissa sputters out a snort-like laugh. Of course she would leave the answering to me.

"Cohen, we talked about this the last time you asked for… wiener rings. Let's wait until you're older—way older—before we talk about that one, okay?"

"Okay. Can I have a monkey?"

"How about we stick to the trampoline before we start bringing in zoo animals?"

"Okay. Can we wake up my girls now so we can open up our presents?" He's literally bouncing in his seat.

"How about this? The girls are so small that they aren't going to miss anything if you start, and they can join us when they wake up. How about we go open some of your presents or at least go see what Santa brought before we go wake them up?"

His brow crinkles and he tilts his head to the side before speaking. "Why would I do that? My girls need to be with me. I can wait."

How did I get so lucky?

"You're one awesome big brother, you know that?"

"Yup!"

We finish up our breakfast. Cohen helps Melissa clean up the dishes, and I go check on the girls. I am just about to step through the threshold of their room when I hear my phone ringing from the office down the hall.

Knowing it's either work related or one of the guys, I groan and head off to my office.

"Cage," I bark in the phone.

"My, aren't we happy this morning," Axel laughs in my ear.

"You try having two newborns and a kid who thinks waking

up before the roosters is a brilliant idea."

"Yeah, I've got one of those kids. Nate was up at five this morning. He isn't even old enough to know what the hell is going on, but I swear that kid ran right into the living room and started tearing shit open."

We laugh and continue talking for a few minutes before he gets silent.

"So…Izzy gave me my gift."

"Yeah?"

"Yeah…" He trails off, and I'm not really sure what I'm supposed to say here. Obviously he's calling because he wants to tell me what she got him, but I'm not sure what it could be that warrants a call at seven in the morning.

"I reckon next year I'll get a taste of the early rising kid while trying to keep a baby asleep."

It's early, but it's not early enough that I don't catch his meaning.

"No shit? Congratulations, brother! Another little Reid, huh?"

"Best feeling in the world, Greg. Once Izzy held those little angels of yours in her arms, she dragged my ass home and told me she wanted another baby immediately. So I guess in some weird way I should say thanks for turning my wife into a baby-craving sex maniac."

"HA! Well, I'm happy I could help you out."

"Yeah, yeah. Feels good, you know? Having our kids so close together. Going to make for one hell of an interesting future, seeing these kids grow up together."

"As long as you keep reminding Nate to stay away from my girls, we should all just be fine."

We joke back and forth before hanging up. I take off back down the hall and into the girls' bedroom. Looking over the crib they're still sharing. I see identically beautiful faces staring up at me. It causes my heart to skip a beat and a smile to pull at my lips.

"Good morning, my lovely little ladies! I just talked to your Uncle Axel, but don't you worry. I reminded him that you aren't ever going to be dating so I'm sure he's talking to Nate right now about that."

They keep looking up at me, and I smile, rubbing their heads before going about our routine. It takes me longer than Melissa, mostly because I don't have that magic touch it seems only mothers possess. I keep reminding them that they aren't ever going to date and they're going to stay daddy's little girls for the rest of their lives.

It isn't until later that night that I think about Axel and Izzy's new little baby coming, and I smile when I wonder about the chances that they would have a girl. Knowing Axel and his extreme protectiveness over Izzy, it's going to be funny as hell to watch him with a daughter.

"You ready for bed?" Melissa drops down next to me and reaches over to turn off the news.

"Beauty, if you're coming with me, then hell yeah. Way I see it, I've got about two hours before someone is waking up for more food. That's a lot of time to spend between these legs."

She smacks my arm but doesn't waste a second, jumping up and rushing to our bedroom.

I don't get two hours that night. Nope, my girls decide to sleep a little longer. I spend the next four hours worshiping my wife and remembering each and every time just how lucky I am to have this life.

15 YEARS LATER

Cohen

"**I** CAN'T BELIEVE you're leaving tomorrow. At least Lyn and Lila are driving now, so it won't be so bad not having you around to take us places." Danielle looks over at me from the other side of the couch, giggling softly and knowing damn well she's going to miss more than my driving them around.

I throw the game controller down next to me and look over at her. God, she really is beautiful. I should feel guilty feeling these thoughts about her. She's my little sisters' best friend, practically family. Hell, her brother IS my best friend. It's a line I shouldn't cross. God, that makes me feel like such a sicko. I feel like all I do lately is remind myself I shouldn't be lusting after her. She's just about to turn fifteen and I'm leaving to start my freshman year at the University of Georgia.

But I can deny it all I want. There's a connection I've always felt between us—wanted or not.

There's nothing normal about what I feel for Danielle Reid.

"So that's all I am to you? Huh, Dani? Just a ride from point A to point B?"

She blushes, and I swear I feel it all the way to my dick. I should be ashamed for feeling this way about it. For craving this girl as much as I do. I should be out running around town and sinking inside of all the chicks who want to send me off to school in style.

Hell, I'm no damn saint, which really makes me feel like I'm never going to be good enough for Dani.

Plus, her father would kill me.

Not just kill me. He would kill me and my family would never find the body.

Yeah, Axel Reid is a man who I've always known would tear apart anyone who tried to touch his daughter.

"No, Co… You're more than that. A lot more than that." She blushes again and looks away quickly.

Uh, say what?

"Dani? I'm no good at reading between the lines. I might have two little sisters, but unfortunately they never taught me much about how y'all's minds work."

She looks over at me, her green eyes bright with emotion, and clears her throat a few times, pushing her long raven hair behind her ears before talking. I can see the nervousness rolling off of her tiny body.

"Can I be honest with you, Cohen?"

"Oh course, Dani. You know that."

Her eyes widen when she hears my sisters start yelling from upstairs. It won't be long before they fly down the basement stairs to where we're sitting like two twin tornados of sass.

"If you don't want those two overhearing you, now would be a good time, Dani."

She blushes more. "I'm going to miss you, Cohen. I know you don't look at me like I look at you, but one day, you're going to come back and I'll still be waiting for you. Waiting for you to see me like I see you. Mark my words, Cohen Cage. One of these days, you're going to be mine. And until you're ready...I'll be here. I'll be waiting."

Before I can even get a breath in my lungs to respond, Frick and Frack come running into the room, talking about who knows what. I just sit there frozen, my jaw slack and my eyes on Dani. Before I know it, they're pulling Dani off the couch and running out the back of the house.

What the hell just happened?

THE END

Coming next for the Corps
Security series is Asher & Chelcie's
story, COOPER, coming Summer
2014.

ACKNOWLEDGEMENTS

I'm going to keep this short and sweet this time. (Yeah, right!)

First and foremost, to my husband and daughters. Thank you for putting up with my own special brand of crazy while I'm in the middle of writing a book. You put up with a crazy messy house, my moments of complete space-outs and comatose mornings after bring up all night working. I don't know what I would do without you guys.

To the best damn PA in the world, Danielle Calcote. Without you, I honestly don't know what I would do. You keep me from needing one of those fancy straight jackets. #SJ Thank you, from the bottom of my cold heart, for everything that you do for me day in and day out. Don't let this go to your head... but you pretty much are always right. (I can hear Lara yelling at me now for feeding that ego)

Mickey Reed – Girlfriend, you are a gem! You took me in, fixed my mess, and handed him back with a beautiful bow. Your notes are invaluable and I'm looking forward to where we go next.

Now, forgive me for not letting you edit this. ;)

To my betas, my team of kick ass ladies that help make my books better and better. I love you ladies more than you could ever know. Danielle, Debi, Amber, Elle, Becky, and Lara. THANK YOU, I love you all!

Katie Mac. I'm not really sure I could ever thank you enough. You held my hand and love me like one of your own. I love you to pieces.

Melissa Gill – I still don't know how you can handle my insane mind. LOL! I'm so lucky to have you as my graphic queen. All you need is a few seconds chatting and you deliver an image/design like you plucked it straight from my head. And you put up with my crazy PM's throughout the day and all hours of the night. Hehe! <3

Brenda Wright, Oh, B! Book four and you're still by my side and I know I'm lucky as hell to have such a great friend in you. You never stop showing me just what it's like to have a real friend willing to drop anything to help. I love you!

Angela, Katie and Kelly – Really... do I need to express the ways I love you? HA! You girls have been with me from the beginning and beyond that. I couldn't imagine doing this without y'all and our daily messages... and facebook stickers, those really are a must.

Debi Barnes, Jessica Adams, and Julie Bales – thank you for letting me pick your brains about twins! <3 <3 I'm sure it's completely normal to get random messages asking about your sex life while pregnant! (Julie – I totally love you in a way that is probably lesbehonest.)

Heather Horton – You made preemie research so much easier! Thank you for sharing your story with me!

Dr. Erin Ricker – Thank you!! I love that I was able to get help from you with my doctor research! Who would have thought, 28 years ago playing Barbies and listening to Paula Abdul that we would be here! HA! Thank you so much for helping with all the medical questions!!

To the bloggers, reviewers, authors and readers that take the time to read my books. Every review, message and post means the world to me and I can't thank you enough for continuing on my crazy train. <3 <3 <3

My street team, for believing in these boys and me. You're pimping and encouraging means the world!

Chelcie, I love you. So much. True friends are hard to find, but we found each other and I'll be forever thankful for that.

To the girls of the IRAC. Do I have the right words to express my love for you? Nope, I do not. But, I will say that our group is amazing and each day you ladies show me just how lucky I am to be apart of it.

And to everyone that loves Greg, Melissa, AND especially Cohen Cage as mush as I do…This book is for y'all.

My readers rock…I'm so blessed to have y'all in my life and I can't thank you enough for loving my Corps Crew as much as I do. Until next time…MUUUUAH

EXCERPT FROM

FALLEN CREST HIGH

BY TIJAN.

MY HANDS clenched the gas nozzle tightly and I couldn't take my eyes off of him.

Logan Kade, my soon-to-be-roommate. While I watched through the window, he laughed at something his friend said. Lydia and Jessica saw who was in the other aisle and quickly went to flirt with them. The friend looked interested, but Logan skimmed a bored eye over them and went back for something more inside the store.

I hadn't seen the Kade brothers up close, not in a long time, but I'd heard plenty about them. Logan was a junior, like me. Mason was a year older. Both were good looking and Mason was rumored to be six foot one with a muscular build. He played defensive lineman for a reason on his football team. Logan had the leaner build, but he was an inch shorter.

I snorted to myself. I couldn't believe I even knew these details. As I cursed my friends inside for their gossiping ways, I glanced back at the Escalade and froze once more. Two green eyes stared back at me.

Mason had been filling up his vehicle and watching me the whole time.

I swallowed painfully and was barely aware that my gas was done. I couldn't look away from him.

Logan was handsome. There was no doubt about that, but he had nothing against his older brother. Now I understood why so many gossiped and whispered about the Kade brothers. The hairs on the back of my neck stood straight up and my eyes were locked with his in some sort of battle.

I couldn't look away. I just knew that.

His friend rounded the vehicle and leaned beside him. Both watched me and I saw the grin come to his friend. He crossed his feet and looked like he was at the movies, popcorn and all.

Then he said something and Mason smirked at me.

"Mase, dude. Candy flavored condoms." Logan leapt across the lot and did a small dance when he handed a box to his brother.

I knew I shouldn't have been watching, but I couldn't stop myself. I was riveted by both brothers. Logan was bobbing his head in rhythm with the music that blared from the gas station's speakers while Mason hadn't taken his eyes from mine.

That's when I knew without a doubt that he knew who I was.

I sucked in my breath and my knees trembled for a moment. What'd I do? Did I do something? Then I remembered my mom sitting in between all those boxes, tears down her face, and an empty bottle of wine beside her.

Fuck them. And fuck their dad.

My mom wasn't a saint. I knew that for sure, but she'd been with my dad for the last seventeen years. Now she cheated? Now she decided we should move in with her new boyfriend and his family?

Fuck them all.

My eyes hardened. Mason's narrowed. I sneered at him before I went inside to pay. When I came back out, Lydia and Jessica were still in the bathroom; Mason passed me to pay inside. He wore a black leather jacket over a black shirt and jeans. His black hair was cut short and his eyes held mine in some form of trance as he passed by me. His jacket rubbed against me, he passed so close, and we both turned to watch the other.

My heart faltered for a moment.

The same hatred I felt for him was in his eyes.

Fuck him.

I lifted my lip to sneer at him and I knew he read the message because he narrowed his eyes, but shouldered inside the store.

I sighed and went to my car to wait. Logan and their friends were inside the Escalade, laughing about something. Then the door pinged its exit and I stiffened. I knew who'd be coming again.

I looked, I couldn't help it, and met Mason's gaze as he neared me. He paused, close to my car and looked like he was going to stop. I lifted my head up, ready for whatever he was going to lay on me, but two cars screeched to a halt not far from us.

His eyes snapped up. "What the hell?"

"Hey losers!" a guy yelled and cursed at them as he ran from the car with something smoking in his hand.

"Oh hell!"

"Mason!"

Logan and their friends were out of the car in an instant. Mason rushed past me and I stood there, shocked, as all four dragged the guys from the other cars. Logan grabbed the smoking thing from the guy's hand and gave it to his brother. Mason took it and threw it in the first car. And the rest of the doors were flung open. Guys from that car poured out. Then another smoking thing was produced and Logan flung it into the other car.

Their two friends were still punching some of the other guys. Mason and Logan started punching the rest. It wasn't long before the cars were filling up with smoke and I got the first whiff of fire.

"Oh no," I muttered to myself and dashed to the store. After I flung open the door, I screamed, "Lydia, Jessica, get out here now!"

They rushed from the back section and stared, dumbfounded at me. "Sam, what's going on?"

I latched onto Lydia's arm and dragged her out with me. "We're leaving. Now."

Jessica followed behind, but braked in the middle of the lot. Her eyes were wide as she took in the sight before her.

I shoved Lydia inside the car and twisted around. "Get lost! The cars are going to explode."

Mason and Logan's friends heard me and stopped. They grabbed Logan first, but all of them dragged Mason away from the guy he was punching. Fury lit up his face, but when Logan said something in his ear, he turned and leapt for his Escalade. As he climbed inside, his eyes met mine for a second.

EXCERPT FROM IGNITE BY TESSA TEEVAN

I *FUCKING hate you sometimes…*

The words replay in my head as if on loop. Like I've died and gone to Hell, where I'm tortured with those five cruel words over and over again. The words that came from the same lips that used to whisper "I love you" as he held me in the middle of the night. The lips that, at one point, couldn't wait to say "I do." Those beautiful lips I thought I'd spend the rest of my life kissing. "I fucking hate you…" Yep, definitely Hell.

Hell on Earth, that is. I'm still here. He's the one who's gone. The love of what I thought would be my life, the man I married, the one I was so sure I'd wake up to every single morning until the good Lord decided to bring me home. The same man, who, on what was unknowingly his last day, spoke those five heartless, torturous words he will never, ever get the chance to take back. That man's gone, and I'm still here, broken and alone.

I'm not a complete idiot. Just an overly dramatic one at times. I know my husband loved me. He'd loved me for more than seven years, and that didn't change. We just spent the morning lying in bed for a few extra minutes so we could be close. He fingered my hair as he told me he loved me and was looking forward to the weekend getaway we had planned. He wasn't going through the motions; he meant every word as he gave me a preview of what he had planned for our downtown Chicago hotel—if we ever decided to get out of bed and hit the road. It's just that I can be a raging psycho when I'm PMSing. Then throw in a wine hangover and I turn into Satan's worst nightmare. Every month it's either intense cramping for four days or my husband wonders where this crazy bitch stashed the sweet woman he married. Suffice it to say, I was not cramping this month.

I understood his frustrations with me when I was like that, and any other time I would've just ignored those words because I usually deserved them. I knew he'd end up doing something to make me laugh in the moments that followed because neither of us could stay mad for long. This was different. He'd never used the word hate before. It caught me by surprise, and at the time, I was extremely thankful for the sunglasses on my face as I looked out the window at the fields of towering windmills on the Indiana countryside.

Hate. I *hate* onions. I *hate* Ohio drivers in the winter. I *hate* anything sparkly-vampire related.

I hate a lot of things, I really do, but it's a strong emotion I only use when thinking about trivial things. My husband, though? Never, not once, have I ever felt hatred towards him, and it tore me in two to hear him say those words. And what's worse is that I'll never hear him say anything again.

We never did make it to Chicago. I don't remember much

about that accident. Actually, I don't remember the accident at all. A car accident. I used to think that was so cliché. Couldn't life be a little more creative? And now, here I am, widowed at twenty-six because of a damn car accident I have no memory of, only splotchy nightmares that just give me snippets of what happened.

The eye witness and police reports say that a young college student was running late to get onto the Purdue campus for his early afternoon classes. He cut us off, clipping the front end of our car. We ended up spinning into oncoming traffic where we were hit by an SUV on the driver's side. He was killed instantly. I was knocked unconscious. When I woke up the next day in an Indianapolis hospital, I knew.

"Mrs. Tate, I wish we could have done something, but he was killed on impact. Take solace in knowing that he felt no pain…" The doctor continued, but his words were drowned out in my mind, replaced by others.

I fucking hate you sometimes.

Excerpt from

Push the Envelope

by Rochelle Paige

FLOWERS...CHECK.

Chocolates...check.

Champagne chilled and ready to go...check.

Noise-canceling headphones so I didn't have to listen to whatever noises were going to float up from the rear cabin...check.

This was so totally not the normal pilot's checklist. When I talked to Dad over the summer about offering Mile High Club charter flights so we had some extra money coming in to cover my room and board at college, I had no idea how the idea would take off. I'd figured I would take a couple flights out each month so Dad wouldn't have to scrimp on anything so that I could live on campus. He really wanted me to get the whole college experience, especially since I had chosen to stay in town for school.

Who knew there were so many middle-aged housewives looking to spice up their marriages? I usually had three to four flights booked each week now. At a cool grand per booking, we made enough to cover my room and board and maintenance on the planes, and we even had money left over to pay off my student loans and to cover my tuition for my next two years. I guess they're right when the say sex sells!

Since the flights were offered in the evening, they didn't interfere with my classes. Dad wanted as little to do with this venture as possible. He had told me that this was my idea, and he expected me to run with it. Talking about anything connected to sex with his daughter wasn't really high on his list of things to do. I figured I was lucky that he was willing to let me use the Cherokee for the flights. I just had to make sure I booked them when I was able to be in the pilot's seat. The last thing I wanted to do was screw my grade point average over because I was skipping too many classes to pilot the flights I was only offering so I could pay for school in the first place.

Today's flight was due to depart in about thirty minutes, so the lucky couple should be here any minute now. I needed to get my butt in gear so I would be ready when they arrived. The plane was set up for their romantic rendezvous. I was dressed in my charter pilot gear of loose khaki pants and a Hewett Charters polo shirt. I'd pulled my long brown hair back in a low ponytail. This appearance seemed to help the wives feel more comfortable with the idea that their pilot was a twenty year-old girl. Add into the equation that I am passably attractive and I could have a problem on my hands with my paying customers. So I did what I could to make sure I presented myself as a capable pilot and nothing else.

I know it's crazy for some people to picture me piloting a plane, but I started flying with my dad before I ever got behind the wheel of a car. He lived to fly and taught me to love it as well. I had my permit when I was sixteen, earned my private license when I was seventeen, and got my professional license when I turned eighteen. Some days it felt like I spent more time during my life up in the air than I did on the ground.

Yet another reason Dad wanted me to live on campus this year—so I could hang out with girls and act my age. Dad and I had been two peas in a pod forever, and now he worried that I needed to have a normal life with girlfriends, parties, and boys. I admit that my upbringing wasn't exactly orthodox, but I was happy with the way things were. I just wished Dad would understand that.

Damn, it sounded to me like my housewife of the day had gone all out for this trip based on the click of her stilettos hitting the tarmac. I didn't understand how women could walk on shoes that looked like skyscrapers to me. Guess that was just the tomboy in me, much to my best friend's dismay. Time to get my head in the game so I didn't scare off the paying customers.

"Welcome to Hewett Charters," I greeted the middle-aged couple as they made their way towards me. "You must be Mr. and Mrs. Williams?"

"Yes, that's us," tittered the platinum-blond woman as her husband looked at me quizzically. I guessed that she hadn't used their real name in the hope that they could keep their trip private. She needn't have had that concern since I offered complete confidentiality.

"Thank you for booking your flight with us today," I said. "Everything is all set, and we can be in flight as soon as you are ready to go. Did you have any questions before we board?"

"Ummmm, are you our pilot?" asked Mr. Williams.

"Yes, I'm Alexa Hewett. Don't worry. You're safe with me. I've been doing private sightseeing tours for a couple years and have had my pilot's license for almost three years. I might be a little young, but I grew up with my dad in the cockpit of a plane. I can assure you that I am fully qualified to take you up," I answered.

"And how does this work exactly?" he questioned.

I couldn't help but smile at the question. It seemed that the wives always booked these flights, and the husbands always seemed uncertain once they got here. I even had flights where the husband had no idea that his wife had booked the tour with the sole purpose of getting it on mid-flight. The expressions on their faces when they saw the bed in the cabin were priceless. It kind of cracked me up since I always figured guys were less shy about sex. Which may still prove to be true since I hadn't seen a single guy yet turn down the opportunity offered by my special charter flights.

"If you will follow me this way, you can see how we've set the Cherokee up so that you will have plenty of room in the rear cabin. Once we are in flight, I will draw the privacy curtain and wear noise-canceling headphones during the flight. I will be able to communicate with the tower but won't be able to hear anything from the cabin. Any of your activities while on board will be as private as possible." They both nodded and looked at each other while blushing.

I walked the couple towards the plane, showed them the bed area we had fashioned by removing four of the seats, and asked them to sit in the rear-facing seats during takeoff for their safety. If the hot looks they were flashing each other as they buckled up were any indication, they were ready to go.

"Enjoy the refreshments, and I will let you know when it is safe to move about the cabin," I said as I got settled into the cockpit.

As I prepared for takeoff, I couldn't help but chuckle to myself about the irony of me helping couples to spice up their sex lives. I wasn't exactly qualified to do so except for piloting the plane. I couldn't really be described as very experienced in the bedroom. Yet, I have turned my beloved Cherokee into the equivalent of a by-the-hour hotel room.

Made in the USA
San Bernardino, CA
26 July 2014